ENGAGED TO LIBERTY

ENGAGED TO LIBERTY

Oscar Rimi

PARTRIDGE

To order additional copies of this book, contact
Partridge India
000 800 10062 62
orders.india@partridgepublishing.com

www.partridgepublishing.com/india

CONTENTS

In the loving memory of Liberty Y. ;
a woman who lived to love her husband and country,
a woman touched by grace for all eternity.

To A.R.S.S. Khan,
for proving that not all heroes wear capes.
Thank you for being human.

*   *   *

Landing in London, Lorraine Venus strolled through the vast airport's arrivals' terminal aware that she had no idea where to go yet. She had no reason to be wandering around, except for the fact that she had shot her fiancé in the leg and could only pack up her bag and run away. She had to get away; from her family, from her life, from him and from the world. Going to Hawaii was not an option because she already had family there, and distant cousins resided further north, so that was out of the question too.

The American girl was dressed in a light blue summer dress that barely touched her knees and black designer heels that exposed most of her white skin but none of that attracted eyes to her the way her long red hair hung around her pretty face, accenting her green eyes and long lashes. Oblivious to those around her, the Texan woman sat down and opened her LV handbag and fumbled through for her wallet, because she needed to get herself a cup of coffee and a bite to eat before she passed out from hunger.

Lorraine searched faster as her stomach growled, her fingers finally finding her wallet and as she clutched it in one hand she grabbed her bag with the other, and got up to order a cup of that strong black drink. Putting her wallet down on the counter she made her order, trying to act casual and ignore the feeling that a pair of eyes were piercing her head from behind. Trying not to act nervous and hoping that she was just being paranoid, the redhead refused to turn around and find out who was burning holes in the back of her head. After a few minutes of torture she got her coffee and sandwich and hurried away from the counter to the same seat she had occupied earlier pretending to sweep her eyes casually across the hall. When the first time got her no familiar faces, she relaxed and turned to her hunger issue and resolved it. When she was about finished, Lorraine rolled her remaining drink around in the cup contemplating whether to finish it and leave the hall or get another cup.

Half an hour later with two more fresh cups of coffee in her belly, she ventured walking around still clueless as to what she would do or where she should go. She couldn't go back home, *not yet.* She had to spend a week away at least to get her fiancé out of her mind. *Son of a wench!* Three days before her wedding he admits to cheating on her with her colleague. If she hadn't caught him she might never have known and after all she wished she had never known. She closed her eyes trying to keep her tears from flowing and her mind focused on her situation. Chad Venus, her brother, would take care of it; he would know the truth and clear things up in his own way so that that jerk would file no lawsuit against her. After all that her family had done to get the wedding preparations in order in just two months as per the in-laws' wishes, with working so hard and having little time for their own, he turned out to be garbage. If love was a highway, she guessed that he had found his exit a long time back, but she still couldn't understand why it effected her so much. She didn't need to know now that he had paid for it with that bullet, and to her that was justice for now. She was Lorraine Venus, no one played around with her when it came to her feelings.

She thought with despair of the client's files piled on her desk at the law firm. She had delayed everything thinking it would still be there when she returned from her honeymoon and had her partners deal with the urgent cases, but now she wished she had done her job and left him to wait. When she had had enough thinking and brooding over her past tense of a fiancé, she headed towards the Duty Free for a quick tour and figured that she could maybe buy a book or a magazine to read. Not forgetting the uneasy feeling of being watched, she slowly twirled around the small stalls and jewelry stands, both checking out stuff with her eyes and glancing around strangers' faces smiling politely. The crystal figures in the shops made her smile as she thought of her brother's study and the ornaments he had collected over the years, *he would like one of those,* she thought.

Her interest was quickly captured by the perfume stand she passed by as she went around shelves trying different kinds and sampling even the men's cologne seeking gifts, to move on after that to the alcohol section checking out the racks for her personal favorite. She was just stepping into the book corner when she thought she heard someone call out her name, she halted and turned around quickly to make sure, but still no familiar faces appeared around her. She gulped wondering if she was going crazy, as she turned back to face the magazine stand she found that someone had stepped between her and the magazines she wanted to look at. The thin woman wasn't given the chance to loosen her frown and decide whether to move along or wait, because that person turned around to face her and smiled. A smile that reached the pair of familiar eyes as well showing how amused the man was at the confused look on her face as she tried to place him, and then as recognition slowly showed on her face.

"Vasille.." she said half asking half exclaiming as she stared at the Albanian gentleman, who was standing there dressed in a beige shirt that stretched over his broad chest and loose black pants, his trimmed beard unable to hide his smile. When he finally nodded she laughed in relief, "Oh my God…I can't believe this."

A million questions popped in her mind and were crowding trying to get out of her mouth, but all she could ask is, "Did you just call my name minutes ago?"

Laughing deeply, the tall man answered. "You don't answer to Elle anymore, do you?"

"When in Rome…"

"Yes of course, when in Rome…"

"Yea" she said breathlessly still stunned, "well obviously, you are the last person I imagined to find here."

"I am not here alone though." He answered running his hands over his beard teasing her. "I have company."

"Oh, well is there someone I know?" she asked trying to be hopeful, she could have been destined to be here if the name she was waiting for was miraculously mentioned.

"Well Marroma is here, and Pierre too."

"Marroma??" she asked her heart skipping a beat at the mention of a familiar name.

"We are going to Dubai, to meet with friends. Marroma is going to see her brother Adhnan too. And you, where are you headed?"

"No where really. I am just here." she manged to say as her heart skipped a beat again at the mention of that one name.

"What? So you woke up this morning with the desire to go to London and roam in its airport.

"No," she answered laughing, "my horoscope said that in London I would meet some friends."

"Interesting" He said amused "never really believed in them" putting his hands in his pockets and rocking on his heels.

Laughing she swatted at him with the back of her hand causing the handbag on her shoulder to slip, as she adjusted it she said, "Let's go say hi to Marroma. I have missed her."

With a a smile, her acquaintance stepped to the side, allowing her to walk in front of him through the aisle. Lorraine's mind clouded with memories as her eyes sought the woman who would ease her aching heart and tell her how Adhnan is, the man who was right for her in every way. *Well, except for his religion, nationality and loyalty,* she reminded herself with a sad smile. But that was in the past; he probably moved on from her memory and is married by now, or maybe still engaged with freedom fights. Upon finding the Indian woman and the French journalist, Lorraine was hit by a wave of yearning and nostalgia that she wasn't prepared for. Images of the time she had spent with them several years ago, when she had ran away from home the first time at a younger age, came rushing slide after slide in her mind. As Lorraine approached the table where the two friends sat, the Indian woman stood up and reached over to wrap her arms around the redhead in a warm familiar hug showing how she had recognized her instantly. As the women exchanged greetings in a tight embrace, Vasille and Pierre waited patiently knowing that until the hug was over they couldn't say anything.

When the four of them were seated and hellos were exchanged, Vasille excused himself to get some coffee and came back with hands loaded while the others caught up, and all Lorraine wanted was to discuss was their united past and their friends.

When Marroma mentioned Dubai, Lorraine jumped in and asked about it.

"I'm going to see Adhnan soon." The happy woman answered, "We are meeting for a bit and later we have to fly to France for the surgery."

Alarmed Lorraine asked fearing the worst for him, "What surgery? What's wrong?"

The Asian girl in front of her sat there proudly her dark brown eyes smiling and her shoulder length chestnut hair pulled back by a red headband from her round childish face. She was clad in a pink maternity shirt with lacy sleeves and long frilly maroon skirt, Lorraine hadn't paid attention to the bump that the woman's hands rested on as they talked until the woman reached out and pulled Lorraine's hand to her body the Texan woman gasped with surprise, "You are expecting.."

At that Marroma nodded with a smile, "I am having twins and I might need a surgery."

"Oh honey! Congratulations…I am so happy for you." Lorraine kept on jabbering, hoping that they hadn't noticed her alarm over a man she met years ago.

Then suddenly pausing she asked, "Marroma darling, who's the lucky father to be?"

Pointing to Vasille, Marroma laughed, "We got married a few years back after everything was over, and have settled in France ever since."

Vasille reached for is wife's hand from across the table between them, "That is true; we were the few of who had been blessed."

Turning her face away from the smitten couple, she met Pierre's blue eyed cold stare, the French journalist dressed in dark denims and a light blue polo shirt, gave her a weak smile. She didn't know him that well; they had run into him briefly and even then Adhnan wasn't comfortable around him.

"Where are you headed Elle?" asked Marroma resting her hand on Lorraine's shoulder waking her from her trance.

"No where really" she said with a smile.

"Does anyone call you Elle these days?" Put in the annoying Frenchman.

"Isn't Elle your name?" Marroma asked, not knowing the reason behind Pierre's question.

"Elle isn't her nickname Marroma" explained Vasille to his wife.

Lorraine took the younger woman's hands in her own and said, "My name is Lorraine and not Elle."

Marroma's face didn't show displeasure, instead the woman nodded and said "Oh alright, but then why?"

Nodding Lorraine, squeezed Marroma's hands and said, "But everything else about me is genuine."

Marroma smiled slightly embarrassed at being the only one who had no idea, "I don't know anything about you, save what Adhnan told me."

Even though the red head wanted to know what that man had said about her, she said rubbing Marroma's hand in a friendly gesture, "I will tell you everything. I will tell you the whole story, how about that?"

The pregnant woman nodded with a smile, and Vasille slid down in his seat knowing that this would be a good way to pass the time, not to mention he already knew Adhnan's side of the story so it was a good way to see how bona fide this young Miss, his friend had adored, really was.

CHAPTER 1

Sitting down on a bench under the hot sun one dry afternoon, the American redhead took off her straw hat as she gathered her hair to one side of her neck trying to cool down, looking around for a sign of her brother. Fanning herself with her light hat, she narrowed her eyes into slits as she looked around for his familiar khaki pants, glancing quickly at the time on her expensive wrist watch that matched her designer white short sleeved ruffled shirt and red vertically pleated skirt.

Watching patiently as many men went by, Lorraine Venus knew that her brother would get mad at seeing her here, in Panama of all places and without his approval. She knew he would never have allowed it, but she needed to see him. She would even go home today if she were to find him and talk to him. She was told that this is where he would be stationed; the US army would not send the soldiers into the city itself but in a a set of buildings at the edge of the city called the "Military square", where the five adjoining almost run down buildings incorporating the American embassy, separated the city form the jungle at its back.

She opened her camera and started to clean the dusty lens when the photo album, she had brought along with her to comfort her fell out of the bag and onto the sandy ground. Lorraine bent down to pick it up, keeping a hand on her open bag, then straightening up again slowly she glimpsed the tall figure of her brother and some soldiers in his wake leave one of the brown buildings. She quickly grabbed at the album and her bag and started to get up and call out to him. The Texan woman could recognize her brother from a million miles away by his set jaw and crew cut. The Texan sibling who wasn't far away, turned his head towards his caller and upon seeing her stopped in his tracks, making the soldiers halt abruptly. But before he could make a

1

step in her direction and before she could reach him in her red high heels and full hands, a grenade fell right in the middle of her path.

The American woman stopped in her tracks, looking puzzled at what had seemed to fall from the sky. She was puzzled for a few minutes then recognizing the dangerous object she tried to retrace her steps to avoid being harmed but she was frozen in place, seeking her brother's aid with her eyes. Her brother was already yelling at his men to move back and away in search for its source. Within seconds men in black tops, pants and masks were covering the building grounds aiming and shooting at the Americans who were weaponless in their army greens, all the while Lorraine still stood in her place unable to make a move. She stood there hyperventilating until an arm grabbed her by the waist and hauled her back instants before the grenade finally exploded throwing the nearby men onto the dusty ground.

Amidst the panicked screams of the men in the vicinity, Chad Venus got his senses back and looked towards the charred remains of the bench that his sister had occupied in the yard, standing up and grabbing a stick by his side he aggressively started shouting orders and calling his sister's name afraid that she was caught up in this or worse *dead*.

In the total of ten minutes, the small battle was over leaving no masked men on the scene, none alive, dead or injured, while the American soldiers who weren't so lucky were scattered either hurt or dead. Chad Venus cursed silently as he held his hand to his grazed left shoulder. He ran inside to look for a weapon, grabbing the first rifle he laid eyes on, and without waiting for any report he dashed outside between the yelling men to search forhis sister. The worried Texan searched everywhere kicking down doors and checking out roofs but to no avail. No trace of his sister was found and with intense horror he realized as he stood on top of a deserted café right across the embassy, that his sister had been taken from the scene by the attackers.

He let the rifle fall, letting his guard down knowing that those bastards were miles away with a hostage and were not returning anytime soon. Knowing that he still glanced down from the roof desperately searching for a lead or link to her and he prayed for any little thing, after that grief stricken and numb he made his way back to his office dragging the firearm behind him feeling tired and beaten. Not only were those terrorists confident enough to attack in broad daylight, they were lucky to get away with it leaving nothing behind and taking the captain's sister with them, this thought stopped him in the middle of the yard just as he was going back to the embassy. *I bet that they don't even know that she is my sister, nodding relieved, if they believed that she was an innocent bystander they wouldn't hurt her...oh what the hell were you doing here anyways Lorraine? What could have brought you here?* He wanted to shout out.

"What do you think they want?" asked Major Simms, who was standing calmly by the window talking to Chad who was in his chair behind his desk, his head between his knees feeling weak and queasy. He knew this was going to be a tough situation with the hostage element, his sister that is; he was going to be spinning on his heels 24/24 till it ends.

"No idea." He managed to say between long deep breaths. "Maybe they are unhappy with the new president's hairpiece." Trying to make a joke, since the new president of Panama had only been in his seat for two days.

"What is wrong with you?" asked the Major, "is it your wound?"

"I will be fine. I am just feeling sick to my stomach." both of them knowing it wasn't from the smell of blood or the attack, but his anxiety over his sister's wellbeing. Chad had told his senior his fears the minute the Major arrived but the senior, being an old friend and wise negotiator, concluded that they were a bunch of amateurs according to their method of attack.

Two hours later after being informed, the base provided back up and dispatched resources, while the host country emphasized the gravity of this situation making it a priority because it occurred on Panamanian soil, but Colonel James Tanner involved himself and talked his way through taking control of the search saying that he would come for support. He highlighted the importance of the operation and emphasized the need for precision and out most efficiency since the hostage was an American and one of their own, making it more personal and close to home.

Losing to them wasn't an option, Chad mused as his eyes went over the maps between his hands, yet the places marked with stars, dots and lines passed through his mind as incoherently as hieroglyphics. He closed his eyes and pinched the area between them just above his nose, trying to stay focused even though all he could see was his sister's smile hiding a broken heart. He knew she had come to see him to talk about Laurie, her daughter who was killed six months ago. He had tried to get her to leave the house to move on and get her wound to heal, but she told him that he would never understand how it was for a parent to lose their child to some merciless fate.

He dropped the maps and walked out to get himself a cup of coffee when a rookie walked in with a charred bag in his hands. Chad stopped in his tracks, his insides lurching as he recognized Lorraine's bag. Grabbing it out of the young man's hands, then grabbing the former from the lapels with the other, he half pulled half dragged the stunned rookie to the Major's office, where they rummaged through the bag to find something useful, but all they could find was the album and camera case and her personal stuff, so the hurting man then threw the bag into the rookie's face and barked orders to get prints off it quickly.

Chad sat down, album in hands, knowing what pictures he would find in it even before he opened it. As he started to go through the pictures of his dead niece, the nerves in his temple began to stand out. On one of her birthdays, Laurie posed in a white spring dress with yellow flower print smiling at the camera timidly to hide her broken front tooth. Her blond hair was flowing over her shoulders, simply pulled away from her light colored eyes by a yellow hair band. Another picture showed her with her mother happily hugging each other. When Chad couldn't take it anymore, he closed the photo album grinding his teeth and excused himself to go back to his office.

Meanwhile, Lorraine woke up to find herself sitting in a chair, her hands aching because they had been tied behind her back for a while. Closing her eyes for a minute, she took a deep breath and tried to make sense of her dusty empty rundown surroundings and when the minute was over Lorraine's heartbeats started to accelerate, her breath came in short gasps as she started to panic, because her mind was unable to control her claustrophobic nature and failing to keep her calm, everything around her went black again.

When the Texan woman opened her eyes the second time, she wasn't tied to the chair; instead she was sprawled on her side on a couch in a different room, maybe a different place altogether. She waited a few minutes to relieve the stiffness in her body, turning to sit up with the least sound and effort as not to alert anyone in the room, unable to see if she was alone yet. She groaned quietly as she moved onto her side finding it hard at first, then swung her legs slowly off the worn out couch and tried to sit straight clutching her knees. She opened her eyes wider to adjust to the dim room and glanced around her to discover that the room was empty. With a heavy heart and sleepy eyes she scanned the room that contained a small wooden kitchen table with four wooden chairs around it, the red drab couch she was laying on, a TV screen and a rectangular mirror on the wall by the door. The window was shuttered and the drapes were closed so only a few rays of light would enter the room; but she could still find the light switch across the room. She looked up at the neon lights that flickered with her touch to see that they were covered with cobwebs, a sight that made her shiver. She didn't know whether to open the door and run out or to stay put. If she escaped now she would have a high chance of getting away she figured, however she could also be intercepted halfway and get shot down. The reality that she could be in hell was alarming enough, but also with a sickening feeling she acknowledged that she could be miles away from her brother and further away from civilization even. Taking a deep breath she reached for the door but her plan was hindered when she heard voices coming towards her closer and clearer, her heart beat faster with fear not knowing what to do in case they were coming to kill her. So she quickly switched off the light and sprinted back onto the couch pretending to be asleep, hoping that she could hear something that might help her escape or at least buy her time and save her life.

To her relief the voices passed by her room and walked on, but another reason made her open her eyes in alarm, it was the patter of small steps. Opening her eyes in fear, Lorraine saw nothing, but she still sat up suddenly scared, as it never crossed her mind that they could have a animal! Her hands shaking, sweat breaking on her forehead, and unable to control her fear of dogs, Lorraine stood up and walked the length of the room without a second thought. She peeked out of the door and upon seeing nobody, she slipped off her shoes and tiptoed out onto the corridor and down the wooden steps to the floor below. Looking to her left, she saw a big window, walking to it as quickly as she could without making a sound, she looked out and her mouth fell open. Just below a lush mass of trees spread for miles and beyond that was nothing but desert land. Not losing hope, she trotted back to the steps and kept going down till she reached the ground floor; she searched for the main door and saw the exact same view from that point as well. Not finding any foreigners anywhere armed or otherwise she made her way around the building and then away into the orchard hoping to find a road that takes her away from this place but yet not strand her in the godforsaken land.

Winding her way among the trees with her shoes back on, Lorraine tried to wind her way through the orchard her heart pounding, nervous while attempting her escape. She was half glad that she was outside the building, and half scared not wanting to believe that there was nothing but desert for miles and miles around this dwelling. When she heard a branch snap somewhere behind her, Lorraine stopped midway the hairs on the back of her neck rising slowly as she heard the cocking of a gun. Unable to move or turn around, her brain incapable of receiving or sending signals, Lorraine's body froze because she knew that a sudden gallop towards the far end of the grove would definitely be suicide. Gathering her courage and holding back her tears, the

Texan woman turned around with her hands up to face the figure behind her, then her knees started to shake when she found herself looking into a man's ugly scarred face. A shrilled scream slit the air, not recognizing it as hers until the menacing looking man standing there took a step towards her in an effort to grab at her hands, and with the same incentive that made her scream, she leaped out of his grasp and towards the fence that separated the orchard from the desert, hoping to make it there, in one piece.

CHAPTER 2

The tall dark haired Indian man, Adhnan, was hauling boxes in the back when he heard a scream rip through the silent afternoon. Placing the one in his hands down slowly as not to move its contents, he sighed and hurried out towards the room where they kept the girl he had saved from the explosion. He had been expecting some drama because the Columbian home owner showed disapproval upon seeing Adhnan walk in with that girl in his arms. She had lost consciousness when the grenade had exploded, and he was obligated to take her in. He had explained to his mates that he wasn't there to hurt civilians, and that he wasn't there to damage property and repeatedly reminded them that he wasn't a terrorist or a rebellion, he was just a messenger.

Reaching her room, he found the red couch he had laid her on empty and a scan of the room showed nothing except for the two cats under the kitchen table. Leaving them behind, he ran down the steps two at a time, stopping for a minute to rest his lame leg. He finished his descent, with his strong leg taking the lead bringing him closer to the main door with each step. He stopped again cursing his leg, grabbing at his throbbing thigh massaging it while his eyes sought the American woman. Then he spotted Quasi, the scarred face garden caretaker who resembled Frankenstein in a modern way, carrying the poor girl towards the house. The man held her by one big arm against his chest, not bothered by her kicking and screaming to be put down, his other arm dangled by his side holding his gun.

The young Asian man walked towards them wiping his hands on his faded black jeans that matched his plain black tank top and black hair. He put his hands up for the big man to put the girl down and when that happened she stopped yelling and screaming but continued to stare at him, as if she'd never seen a human before. He saw that she had put up a big fight, it was apparent by the rips in her assailant's shirt and by her dirt stained face.

Adhnan shook his head impatiently at the big man in front of him, after which he spoke a few words in a language that Lorraine did not understand. He then held out his hand for her with a straight face, and once the hulk behind her let go she walked involuntary to hide behind Adhnan's back not wishing to see the scary man's face again. When her attacker walked away back to his work, Adhnan turned towards the scared girl who looked pathetic with her shirt ruffled and her shoes missing. He reached for her hand but flinching she stepped back, he didn't try again instead he dropped his arms and walked on towards the main house door expecting her to follow him. Instead of that doing that the strange girl turned around and ran off the way the scarred man had brought her winding through trees determined to get out of this place. Staring after her in disbelief, Adhnan stood fixed in place for a few seconds before registering that he should get her before Quasi did. Starting off after her, the young man was hoping that she wasn't a hard headed girl, or else Quasi would never get out of his hair, not even anybody for that matter.

Meanwhile Lorraine ran fast on the prickly ground and small pebbles, without considering the consequences. She was tired, hungry and cold and scared as hell and more so when that scarred man showed from no where and seized her, she thought that she would drop twenty pounds if she had had them on her. Breathing heavily she made her way through the orchard now lost and confused, hearing leaves crunching and stems breaking under the feet of her pursuer, but she was unable to stop choosing to die shot in the back than at that man's hands. That was when it occurred to her that she wasn't shot in the back yet or caught, was the man behind her just toying with her knowing he was going to catch her and torture her anyway. When she glimpsed a metal meshed fence a few yards ahead, a smile broke over her dirtied face but no sooner had she let her guard down than a strong hand reached out and grabbed her by the elbow jolting her to a stop. Lorraine didn't need to look back to see the man in black pants holding her at an arm's length. Raising an eyebrow at her, Adhnan asked her a question as he shook her, but she didn't flinch thinking *he's probably wondering if I am stupid.* But he didn't wait for her answer as he kept a hand on her arm and dragged her towards the house, however she gave him a hard time pulling away yelling at him to let her go. Then stopping for a second he turned around smiling, he put a finger up asking her to wait a minute then let go off her arm and knelt down to turn a stone then stood up pointing for her to look down at her feet, when she did she screamed so loud that she nearly burst her own eardrums. The sight of scorpions coming out from under the upturned stone made her jump quickly into the stranger's embrace with her arms around his neck and her bare feet up in the air. When she reacted like he had hoped she would act, he quickly put his arms around her and treaded heavily in his boots towards the house.

Admitting defeat, Lorraine let her head fall on the stranger's shoulder telling her self that she would eventually try again, but not bare foot that was for sure. She sat there on the red couch in the same room she woke up in, huddled with her knees underneath her not wishing to talk to anyone, not even when her shoes were brought to her. She wanted to know where she was but figured that they didn't understand her language so she saved her energy. However what she wanted to do was eat, a realization coming about when her stomach growled loud enough for the man who was watching her to raise his eyebrow at her one more time, his black eyes twinkling with amusement.

She eyed him as he took out a cell phone and called someone, his lean arms bare, muscles bulging in the right places and long lean pianist like fingers at their ends. His upper body wasn't big but the way it narrowed at his waist was visible, his long legs hidden by his pants and untied boots were possibly as muscular as his arms she thought. Her eyes went back to his face, his chin covered by a day's growth of beard as dark as his mane, his black eyes surrounded by thick black lashes and thick eyebrows complementing his fair skin. A flutter from his eyelashes brought his gaze to meet hers causing a hot flush to play on her cheeks as she turned to look away, embarrassed that he had caught her studying him with curiosity of a stranger.

He watched her as she huddled up on the couch pouting; unable to hide his smile as he wondered what he would do with her. Looking at her bare legs he figured he should first get her something to cover herself to save his sanity.

She watched as he left the room with a frown on his face, *where was he going?* She wondered. *Would he really get me something to eat or leave me to die? Not that I would eat anything they'd offer, they might poison me or feed me horrible things to torture me!*

She placed her head in her hands trying to come to terms with the horrible near future that awaited her or maybe the lack of it, she thought with dismay. When he had taken too long to come back she stood up and walked to the mirror to wipe at the face staring back at her. Appalled at the mud stains found on her face mixed now with her tears, she ripped off the ruffles that had been already torn off her shirt and wiped at her face cleaning as much as she could. As she was using her spit to clean her face, he walked in with clothes in his hands. She didn't notice him standing there watching her childlike actions. When he realized that he couldn't stay still any longer he cleared his throat and stepped in pretending not to look at her, but as he walked across the room the thrill of being responsible for another being sent a strange sensation gliding down his body making him shiver.

CHAPTER 3

He left the room again and she assumed it was for her to change when she saw the garments he had left on the couch. She grimaced as she fingered the rags but decided that the pair of pants she held where better than her skirt. Sliding the harsh material over her skin she kept her eyes on the door in case someone came in, as she zipped up the wide horrible pants and unzipped her skirt, she sighed. She had to get out of this place as fast as she could. Picking up her skirt from the floor, she folded it and placed it on the couch. As the distressed girl turned towards the shuttered windows confusion and fear crept over her wondering if she was really trapped. Tears brimmed in her eyes throwing her off guard, unable to stop herself from feeling miserable.

The dark haired man returned with food interrupting her break down. She held her breath with her back to him as he placed the fruits he brought on the table, and some bread loafs. Her stomach growled at the smell, her mouth watered and she couldn't help but turn around. He pulled out a chair and looked up to her beckoning her with his head. At that she obeyed and took her place at the table to start eating, thinking she had better eat well while it lasted for the next meal could be her. Halfway through her apple, the stranger walked to the windows and unlatched the panes and shutters opening them wide enough to show how the desert outstretched over and beyond. Refusing to think of the situation she was in, or let gloom take her over again, she promised herself that she was going to fight and get out of this hole if it was the last thing she does. She forced a smile as she calmly swallowed her food.

As she was about to start executing her calmness plan, footsteps bounded towards them. When she saw the stranger's frown slowly creasing his face, she knew she wasn't going to be anywhere near calm.

She stood up trusting her instincts and eying the knife the stranger had left on the table, afraid of what was about to go down in a few minutes.

When the scarred man entered the room with another two strangers, Lorraine stepped back in the direction of her dark haired savior to stand behind him as the three men at the door eyed her with criminal intent. The scarred man was dressed in a white and red horizontally striped shirt, apparently small for his bulging muscles, the sleeves barely covering them. His jeans were ripped and torn at the knees and faded everywhere else, his hair a mess. If she had known it was safe to laugh at that ridiculous sight she would have.

The man on his right had a clean look, and was dressed in a white grease stained shirt and dark wide pants, but sharp handsome features and a broad jaw stretching his white skin. His body was fit, lean and accented by his tall frame. The third man wasn't as handsome but was better looking than the scarred man, his fair hair was barely visible under his turned back dirty cap, wearing dark jeans with a white tank top, his bulging muscles and broad chest giving him a menacing air, not to mention the shoulder holster that carried two guns.

Lorraine did all she could not to turn around and jump out of the window, for she was faced with one of two horrible fates, die with a heart attack on her way falling down or be killed by those strangers before she could cry out for help. *Well serves me right*, she thought, *I am being punished for not taking care of my daughter.*

And before she could lift her hands in silent prayer, the handsome one stepped towards her savior and started arguing with him, and from the way he threw angry looks at her, she assumed it was an argument because of her. Both men joined in and started advancing towards the man standing opposite them threatening him. The handsome one stepped forward and started pushing the dark haired man pretending to want to reach for Lorraine, but with one swift push the dark haired man pushed his comrade away and stepped between him and the American girl, as if telling him that she shouldn't be touched. The other two men moved back towards the door still waving their fists as if threatening them both, seconds later their steps sounded heavy as they left the scene. When the footsteps died, both men were left facing each other in the room, and to Lorraine's surprise they suddenly relaxed their stances and their faces broke into smiles as they both walked towards each other ending the charade with a handshake. Their smiles were quickly erased when they turned towards their once scared hostage, but who was now tapping her foot on the floor, her arms crossed over her chest giving them an angry stare of her own.

"We are sorry about that," said the dark haired man, "my name is Adhnan, and this is Vasille."

"Oh great! So you do speak English. Good!" She exclaimed relieved, *or was that good?*

Not knowing whether to laugh or cry, she looked at them each one in turn waiting for them to speak. "What am I doing here?"

When they didn't answer she marched to the table and grabbed the knife she had found earlier, and pointed it towards them, "Talk damn it!"

When they didn't, she assumed that they had nothing to say, so giving her self the authority she kept her hands clenched on the knife on the knife taking small steps towards the door. Before she could dash out a small figure sprinted in bumping into her head on sending the Texan girl down, with the knife racing across the floor and away from her. The young girl who had fallen to her knees due to the collision was now getting up with her hand on her head looking dazed. Taking action at once, Adhnan ran forward to get the knife just to be safe.

Sitting up, Lorraine eyed the girl who had thrown her off guard, taking in the girl's young frame clad in a pink cameo short sleeved shirt and gray khaki pants and worn out sneakers. The Texan woman's eyes went up to the face of that body to see big brown eyes, a small nose on a round face framed by short brown bob of hair, curling at the neck touching flushed cheeks.

"Coco. Are you alright?" asked Adhnan as he walked up to her with a hand stretched out to her, at the same time lending a hand to Lorraine to assist her as well. But when the American girl didn't take it turning her head away, Vasille took two big steps towards the American girl and bent down to haul her up by the arms. As the four of them stood there in the middle of the room, a moment of uncomfortable silence washed over. Then as if remembering why she had come Coco burst out, "I heard about what happened at the square. I..." and before she could go on Vasille's cell phone rang and he put up his arm up to stop Coco from going while he answered.

"Keyalee speaking" he started, then he listened attentively to what the person on the other end of the line had to say, interrupting once in a while to say "Yes" and "I know that" as he paced in the room before he hung up and stormed out.

"Vasille!" Adhnan called out then following him, leaving his hostage with the young girl. Not interested in the Texan woman, the girl walked out of the room as if Lorraine was not there, as if not caring whether Lorraine stayed or ran away.

CHAPTER 4

"I see that you are still here." A voice interrupted her daydreams as she stood at the window looking out. Turning around, Lorraine watched as the one called Adhnan grabbed a chair to sit at the table. Hesitating for one minute, the redhead walked to the table and sat herself down wrapping her arms around herself. She didn't ask what had happened and why they had left her alone all this time, but she knew that if anyone was going to be the one to talk or explain or put her out of her misery, it was this guy.

Clearing her throat, she tried once again, "I don't know if I am a hostage or not, or if I am prisoner or a visitor. But if you let me know that would be nice."

His lips curled slightly, "Nicely put. Not so clever though. You are neither and you are free to go, but the only problem is that there is no place for you to go, or let's say if you want to go back to the city, there is no way."

"Okay, but why am I here?" she asked getting more annoyed by the minute.

"You were saved." He answered, being vague.

"As a matter of fact I was fine till I was kidnapped." She stated.

"You were not kidnapped. You were saved." He pointed out.

"From what?"

"The grenade exploding beside you, ring any bells?" he answered calmly reaching out for an apple on the table.

"I was fine. I could have been saved and left there." She answered, showing anger in her tone.

"If I had left you there, you would have being shot." he answered trying not to snap but was glaring at her.

"So it was you attacking us!" she cried scared, standing up fast toppling her chair over.

Realizing what he had said, "Calm down, it's not like that."

"What else can it be like?" she asked horrified.

"It can be a threat only, not an attack to kill." He explained trying to stay calm under her cold stare and offending accusation.

"But there was a grenade used, that's a murder weapon." She said raising her voice and slamming her palms on the table frustrated.

Standing up and imitating her move, scaring her out of her wits he answered her so calmly, "there were machine guns and gas bombs too involved if you must know. Anyways make yourself at home, fare and food are one me," he said and picked up his apple and sunk his teeth in it aggressively once then put it down because his tense jaws didn't help finish it.

When Lorraine regained her wits, she knew that losing her cool was wrong but she wouldn't apologize yet. She would ask him to help her get back to Chad, if he didn't want to then she would definitely find a way, she could trust him not to shoot her in the back if she fled but she wasn't sure about his crew.

"You know what, I might as well take my chances." She said to herself after a slight pause, and without a backward glance, Lorraine left the room and went down the steps. She actually believed him and she knew that there was no way for her to leave but there was no harm in looking around. When she reached the open front doors, she suddenly stopped as she saw Quasi talking to the fair man and felt a stab of fear for her life. But when she went ahead and started walking out they only gave her a careless glance and went back to their conversation.

Turning around the first corner keeping her back to the house white walls, Lorraine took a walk to the back to stay out of the strangers' sights in a way. As she gazed out she felt a sense of dread fill her chest, the house that was fenced by an orchard from one side, was standing on top of a quarry in the back, and had no back wall or fence, which meant that there was no saving whoever fell down there.

No neighbors, no transport, no place to run… Lorraine's sense of dread nestled around her heart and squeezed it tight, thoughts of dying young and alone brought tears to her eyes, not even the thought of being with her daughter gave her peace. Fear made her turn around and run back to the house and up to the room where she had left Adhnan, the Texan woman intended to go back and beg the foreign man to help her get home. She would worry about her image and dignity later, she wanted a warm bath, softer clothes and to see Chad more than anything. But when she got to the room, the dark haired guy had gone, the table was empty and the knife was stuck in the middle of the basket in a red apple. Retracing her footsteps Lorraine ran back down and to the other side of the house looking for him frantically, that's where she found him hauling crates around. She stood there reluctant for a minute, fully aware that what she was going to ask for if granted, would come with a price.

She was working up her courage when he looked up and saw her standing there fidgeting, waving for her to come closer, "even though it is still daytime I think you should stay inside, it's not safe for you to be out here, you never know who may come and see you. And there are wild animals around here too."

"I am fine. That girl lives here doesn't she?"

"No, she doesn't" he answered out of breath.

"Then? Does she come and go?" She asked.

"She comes on a shooting star." He said with a slight smile.

"Interesting, maybe I can catch one of those," her statement shadowing his sarcasm.

"If I send you to the city in any case, where will you go?"

"Don't worry about me, just send me there."

"I will worry about you, I can't let you go. You are my responsibility. So drop it."

"I am not! You don't even know my name."

Frustrated by her nagging, he put down the box from his shoulder and walked up to her and extended his gloved hand and said, "My name is Adhnan Aksarr, what's yours?"

"L…" she started, then stopped feeling stupid for nearly giving him her real her name.

"Elle? Nice to meet you Elle, now that we are acquainted, let me protect your highness from this panama desert." Dropping his extended hand, he started to turn away but the look in her eyes made him stand still. "What are you still standing here for?"

"I don't need this now, I am going. I would rather be eaten by hyenas than be used by a terrorist like you."

A flash in his eye made her regret her last words, "You know," he started, "for a victim you are pretty dumb and rude. Go on get the hell out of here and for your information we are no terrorists but your white apparently spoiled backside wouldn't know a hard working civilian if he…" Adhnan stopped mid sentence catching him self from saying something he shouldn't so he let it go.

It was in that minute that the angry girl started to turn around and walk away, to find the handsome man come her way his shirt dirt stained, and without a word he grabbed her arm and caught her in place, fury radiating from his eyes.

"Mia's camp was attacked!" he yelled at his friend, unable to control him self Vasille pushed the Texan woman into Adhnan's embrace nearly knocking them both down.

"She called me…they were at their posts." Adhnan said as he regained his breath and steadying the American woman at the same time.

"That was what I thought. It failed! The operation failed. They bombed everywhere! We must go to them…" Vasille exclaimed in short breathless sentences. Falling to his knees the devastated man let out his grief silently for a few minutes wanting to ask Adhnan for some men, but instead Adhnan pulled his friend up and put his arms around his friend comforting him as he sobbed out his heartache.

"Why did I send her with them? Why?"

"let us go to them brother…" Adhnan could only say to calm his friend down. "Where is Coco?"

"I don't know." Vasille answered quietly still in shock. "I don't know."

"Let's go…i will call Marroma for back up" Adhnan took Vasille's arm over his shoulder half hauling him to the front of the house, where they were intercepted by the other men.

Seeing the calm anger in their comrade's walk, the men shook their heads in silence and followed him towards the house's entrance without one backwards glance at Lorraine.

Amazing… I'm not even being watched, Lorraine thought suddenly feeling worthless. *If I was not that important, why wasn't I left alone?* Looking around, the discarded girl didn't know whether to follow the men, or start on her way in her ugly borrowed pants and high heels. Her wondering eyes hit one of the open crates and she thought she might as well take a look.

But before she could, Adhnan came back for her and signaled for her to go in quickly, and all she could do was raise her arms in surrender and walk ahead of him chiding her self for that early thought, apparently this was a hyena she would find hard to escape from.

CHAPTER 5

Lorraine sighed as the desert's tenants huddled together like a pack of wild animals, obviously grieving with Vasille. It wasn't enough she didn't speak their language, and now something had happened and she was left feeling left out and lonely. She'd have to ask Adhnan about it and it was something she wouldn't do but then again she was scared and curious.

When he had separated himself from the pack she slowly edged her self away from the table that she had glued herself to and followed him inaudibly out of the room, hurrying after him as he started to head out to the back, she eventually caught up and stood in his tracks to ask what had happened. He gave her a look which made her wish she had never asked, "Go back inside, please."

"Just tell me." She pleaded.

Without another word, the irritated man pushed her to the side, and the easiness with how she was plastered to the wall surprised her because she wasn't a petite girl, alarmed by his strength she stood her ground and dared not move. It was when he had gone around the corner that she dared follow him. She risked a small peep around the wall to see where he was standing before she walked up to him. The young man was sitting on a crate, smoking a cigarette so she felt relieved that he wasn't working for he could easily haul one of those crates and throw it at her and smash her. She had a feeling that something bad had happened and she had to act compassionate even if she couldn't totally be. She assumed that someone was hurt or missing and to her that was a soul, unidentified, irrelevant but yet a soul. Someone's sister, brother, lover or even friend and it was sad that she felt awful. She clenched her fists as she approached him, aware that his consciousness of her was radiating.

"Didn't I ask you to go inside?" he asked without lifting his head.

"Are you okay?" came her surprising question.

Only then did he left his head up to see her leaning towards him her hands on her knees, her face not far from his. She was startled by the tears in his eyes that she stepped back suddenly nearly falling, but he was fast enough to get up and hold her by her wrist, and being light weight she fell towards him. Without a word he threw his cigarette butt on the ground and put it out with his boots then let go of her wrist and with the fist he had clenched around her tender skin, he lifted her quivering chin to look into her eyes.

"I'm not heartless; I could keep you here for another two years and no one would dare touch a hair on your head. But your people might have killed Vasille's sister and beat the life out of her teenage body. So when you see me in such state listen to me and go back inside."

Taking in every word he was saying, she gulped and put her tearful eyes down, "I am sorry, I…"

"Don't tell me you are sorry sweetheart. I am just protecting you from them, because I brought you here. But I am obligated and stupidly kind at the same time. I will not let them hurt you as revenge but I will not let you do anything stupid, you will not be forgiven if you take my kindness for granted."

Wiping her tears with her thumbs, "You don't get to threaten me. I didn't do anything to you."

"This is not a threat, it is just a reminder."

"How do I know I can trust your people?"

"You don't, but as I said, I will protect you as long as you are good with me. No funny business, no threatening us with kitchen knives. Now go, I want to work"

What she heard him say was that he wanted to be alone so she stepped back but still didn't want to go back inside, "can I at least sit there by the wall?"

"Whatever, just stay out of my way." trying not to get frustrated.

Then before she could object he grabbed her by the waist and placed her into the tree beside him, onto the closest branch. "That way, you will stay away from scorpions and my friends would have to go through me to get to you. Satisfied?" In seconds she got her breath back to thank him sarcastically for being considerate of her safety.

When he got back to his business, she put herself in check. If she hadn't worried or panicked before, this was the time. Vasille was on Adhnan's side and so was that "Coco" girl who sure followed Adhnan's orders, but the other two weren't. Quasi, on his own, would strangle the night and day out of her without breaking a sweat. She stared in space to see the desert, and saw the plain truth, she was a cooked goose. And just like her savior had suggested, if she didn't do funny things she won't end as their dinner. Trying to stay focused and away from her gloomy thoughts, Lorraine contemplated how she'd get to the city before he abandoned her. *What was the worst that could happen,* she wondered, *I would reach the city in a casket or even if I didn't reach a casket I would have still given it my best. Is that what Chad would have done?*

As she thought of her brother, she knew he would never get himself in such a mess. *If* she had told him she was coming he would have provided security. *If* she had not felt sorry for herself she wouldn't have left home. *If* she had taken care of her daughter, all of this wouldn't have happened. So many ifs, but none of what had happened could have been controlled then or changed now. Her daughter died because it was her *fate*, she came here because of *fate*, but her only mistake was deciding to put her brother in a situation that he couldn't get out of. She could imagine him frantically searching, worried about her.

She couldn't trust these people even thought she wasn't particularly the enemy. She had Adhnan on her side, for now and the card he is playing with his mates was "I was the one who brought her here, therefore she is my responsibility", and so far it has saved her hide. Though as much as she hated to admit it, had it not been him who saved her she would still have brought him to her side, because he had a quality about her that she couldn't figure out. He just had "human" sprayed all over and she was ready to use him all the way to freedom. She could play the innocent victim card and she could just become indispensable to him. Not in the sense that he was *obligated* to have her there but in the way that he wouldn't be able to see her harmed. It wouldn't be so tough; after all he was still a man.

She moved in her uncomfortable seat to find a comfortable position as slowly as she could so she wouldn't attract his attention. He looked so engrossed in his work that she didn't even dare poke her nose in his work.

Meanwhile the foreign man stopped his work to glance back at the lady in the tree. She looked so lost in thought that he felt sudden fear tightening in his stomach. She looked like a girl who could do anything she set her mind to and he wasn't about to let her disturb their peace, and blow their cover. He knew since the minute he had brought her in that the dust wouldn't settle in their little vicinity because of her, but he was adamant on not abandoning her. He couldn't concentrate on the task at hand, partly because of her presence and partly because of Mia's situation, both things giving him a headache. In the shadow of a bad mood he hauled a wooden crate too fast, too suddenly that his injured leg cramped and he dropped the box yelling. The minute he fell down in pain, Lorraine was instantly down from the tree tripping in her shoes, rushing involuntary to his side.

"Oh no…Are you okay? What did you do?" she asked afraid that he was hurt bad.

"Nothing." He answered not moving, on the ground on all fours, his eyes red with pain and his jaw set hard. She tried to help him up by bringing his arm over her shoulders but he didn't budge.

"Give me a second." He said whispering. She lowered his arm again and stayed crouched by his side till his stance relaxed and he moved to sit back stretching his legs, still unable to talk; he looked up at her and gave a weak smile when he saw her petrified features.

And in spite of him self he tried to get up reaching out for her hand squeezing it as pain tore through his leg, when that attempt failed he rested back down.

"I will get your friends for you." She said finally and ran back to the house and called the pack of hyenas upstairs. When they hurried to Adhnan, she stood there in the room alone; throwing her arms in surrender acknowledging that her presence here for however long was going to be some sort of a hell. She didn't accept the unfairness, yet she had to bear it for some time. Until the time Chad came to her, and all she could think of was how it was better here than running into the desert and perishing.

CHAPTER 6

Back in the city, while Chad was busy working on any lead to find his sister, Colonel Tanner and his daughter stepped into the distraught man's quarters. Looking up from his desk as the rookie ushered them into his office, Chad stood up quickly to greet and shake hands. The angry, stricken man thanked the Colonel for coming and explained what the urgent matter was, Chad had told the colonel what he could over the phone and the rest had to wait for his arrival.

When Chad finished reporting, the Colonel only nodded then asked, "So what is it that you want, son?"

In any other time, Chad would have asked for his beautiful daughter's hand, but being in this mess Chad wished that this heartless man would soften and accept to help.

"Sir, my sister came to visit me here today but we were attacked and she was kidnapped. I would like your help in finding those savages."

"This isn't about your sister you know, Captain."

"I know sir, but I would very much appreciate finding and getting my sister out of their grip, before we attack and destroy them. So I am asking that I lead this mission for my sister's safety."

"Very well son, just be cautious that your personal issues don't jeopardize the operation. Lives of many men will be at stake so don't let me down." The last words fell on Chad's deaf ears for after he heard the Colonel's approval; Chad's relief was so obvious it made the Colonel's daughter smile. Chad tried not to smile back though his heart was pumping with life at the presence of that angel. He was planning to talk to her about taking their relationship to the next level and proposing to her, but this Lorraine incident would only slow things down. He promised himself that once he found Lorraine he would marry Morena Tanner because he was done waiting and hoping.

After a few more pointers, the Colonel left Chad who was ready to go out and get some work done. He thought that if he was lucky, and she was still held in the city he could find her before midnight, otherwise he would do his best within the upcoming twenty four hours.

As he closed the door behind them, he waited for a few minutes hoping that Morena would walk back in, when she didn't he went back to his desk and picked up his cigarette pack. He tapped the cigarette twice in his hand before putting it between his lips lost in thought, but before his lighter could flicker, the door opened and back in she flew. Dropping the small roll from his mouth as he smiled, he walked to her taking her in his arms burying his face in her neck trying to find comfort and solace. When he looked up, she ran her fingers on his face and assured him that things were going to be okay. He hugged her again, hoping that her embrace would give him more strength; he needed her so much now and was glad she had come back for him. But after seconds she pulled back again and said that she had to go, but he managed to steal a kiss from her before she ran out.

Standing there smiling like a fool, Chad traced his steps and picked up his cigarette, lighting it as leaned against his desk, wondering when she would become his own and when he would get to settle down with her. *But yea, first things first,* he thought, as he left his office his weapons loaded ready for some saving.

While Chad's heart was warmed by the woman of his dreams, his sister's was getting colder by the minute. She had taken the choice to flee that's why when Adhnan was back on his feet, he called out for her but she was nowhere near.

He didn't make a big deal of it until Vasille asked him about her minutes after, Adhnan squinted his eyes in suspicion, "What did you tell her?"

"Me? nothing at all. In fact after she ran to us about you I haven't seen her."

"What about Coco?" he asked still skeptic.

Vasille shook his head indifferently, and that annoyed Adhnan making him run his hands through his messy hair as he walked to the window and leaned over the sill hoping to find her down in the orchard but knew that was false hope.

"If she has run away, she couldn't have gone far. You are bound to find her body tomorrow morning."

"Who said I'll wait till morning?" he answered as he pushed himself back and grabbed his jacket ready to go look for her. But Vasille placed a hand on his friend's shoulder stopping him, "It's getting dark out there and the cold weather will aggravate your wound, also if you're planning to use the bike you will alarm the wolves."

"I can't leave her out there." He said removing Vasille's hand off his shoulder gently. "She is a woman after all."

"She is only trouble for us." Vasille called out after his friend who was already halfway down the stairs. The words fell on his deaf ears as Adhnan ran out to the motorbike he had hidden at the back, putting on his helmet, he revved up the engine and started out not knowing which way she took or where she thought she was going.

Out there in the midst of the desert, the American girl was scared of her wits. Cool winds started to blow through her clothes as evening dropped around her, her insides squirming with fear, trying to tell her self that she wasn't that far and that they were just trying to scare her. She told herself also that a few miles walking in this cold air wouldn't kill her. Her false bravado didn't last long as she stopped in her tracks listening to what was the unmistakable howl of wolves. Lorraine figured she better start running then changed her mind thinking it was better she conserve energy. She looked at her watch and saw that she only had been walking for only one hour, and since she was preoccupied with her destination she didn't notice she was going around in circles. There was no such things as straight lines in the desert, and no such thing as going north without her using a compass. With her mind occupied with surviving this dilemma and what she would do when she reached the city she didn't hear the sound of an engine closing in.

Adhnan spotted the red heels that she had ditched a while back, and then he found her looking around oblivious of the cold weather and silent scary evening, a speck of a human on the horizon from where he was standing but imagined a meal for any wolf combing the area for food. It wasn't until he was a few yards behind her that she turned around and saw him, she sighed sensing there was no running away for her, stood her ground waiting for him.

He closed in and came to a halt in front of her, without turning the engine off; he motioned with his head to her to get on the bike behind him. But she just stood there wondering to herself what would be worse: to go back to these hyenas or let a bunch of wolves eat her? She shuddered at the last thought and he mistook it to her being cold so he took of his jacket and put it around her shoulders pulling her closer, "Come on. We must get out of here." his expression serious.

She looked both ways her mind wheels running, her decision hard to make. But then when she looked at him, she asked, "How far is civilization?"

"A good distance that we can't cross on a bike without having wolves at our heels. So let's go and I promise once I get the opportunity I'll get you to town safe."

Raising her eyebrows, she said, "If you had been decent in the first place you wouldn't have kidnapped me and you wouldn't have had to return me."

Getting impatient with her, he leaned back crossing his arms on his broad chest, "I don't have to do anything and I never said I was decent, I just want to stop the headache I brought onto myself. And nothing would give me more pleasure than to correct my mistake but at this time of day and in this bike it's difficult. Get on now; otherwise I won't be responsible for the state they find your body in."

Clenching her fist outraged by his indifference, "You are such a jerk!"

"Yes, but I am a jerk with good intentions." He answered smiling, "so get on damn it! I am starting to get cold." But when she frowned and shrugged her shoulders, he turned towards her and grabbed her by the waist and hauled her onto the space in front of him, taking her by surprise that she didn't have time to protest.

In the next few minutes, he wrapped her arms around his waist and started back to the house, before the wolves caught up with them, furious at her for calling him a jerk and feeling stupid for having saved her hide again without any appreciation.

CHAPTER 7

After the American girl huddled and went to sleep on the red couch it was after midnight, so the two friends sat at the wooden table to discuss their next step. The young girl, Coco stood as a lookout at the door in case the Columbian duo came up. Even though the men were talking in another language, she could understand them but didn't comment knowing that if her opinion was needed she would be asked and there was nothing to object on yet. She had a problem with the American girl because she was the object of Adhnan's interest now, but she knew that no girl could be suitable for him more than her. She was here to help them stop the Americans from appointing the new president and save the land where she grew up in, as well as be Adhnan's right hand in everything. The comrades were discussing how they were going to move into town without being noticed and settling there to be able to stake out the president's movement. They had to plan it in a better way and have an escape plan in case of contingencies to prevent leaving casualties.

"I don't think all of us should go." She finally interrupted. "Someone must stay here and hold the fort. Someone must be here prepared to save the mission."

"We don't want more people to die. We didn't start this to kill people but for some obvious reason messages are not getting through to people." replied Adhnan

"You know if Adam was here he would have finished off everyone and gotten through with it." Said Vasille, talking about his own older sibling who had worked with them before but had to leave. Unlike Adam who was violent by nature, Adhnan had moved to live in Panama because of his woman and had grown fond of it so they all knew that he didn't come to fight; yet they ended up all living together fighting for the country to became politically stable, by joining riots against the current government to kick out the notorious General Manuel Noriega. The change and disruption of communities by the invading French and American armies aroused the sense of duty, the precursor being injustice inviting rebellion to help regain the identity of the land and return it to the rightful owners; hence "The right to run Panama" or the RRP activists were born.

Adhnan, Vasille, and Coco had joined protests before and had caused chaos in more than one occasion and those incidents helped them find where they belong. With one foot inside the law and one foot out, the threesome found a way to deal with weapons, smuggling them with the help of Quasi and Carlos who owned the orange orchard, the rebels now used as headquarters. Carlos had connections that helped provide weapons, some army help from Mexico and with Adhnan's friend's help from the east smoothed up their work. The legions formed since the upheaval of the resolution turned into armies and flooded like rats from drainpipes that came out from everywhere with stones, rifles, knives, bombs and even bare hands. The years turned panama into a war zone, a war that took place between government and rebels, leaving civilians under their feet, dead or otherwise maimed.

As Coco sat there pondering over their talk, Carlos and Quasi came bouncing up the steps waking her up from her trance. Rushing to sit at the table with the two men she came up with something to talk about as a cover. She didn't know how much she could trust them and her paranoid behavior towards them affected Adhnan's judgment, he needed to trust the people he was around but it was difficult when Coco kept jumping every minute.

Talking to her in simple Arabic, he said, "Stop doing this please, you are distracting me."

"I can not help it. I can not trust them." She answered in her language.

"I can, and I need to. we are a team in this." He said then got up and walked to them greeting them. Knowing that she was rolling her eyes behind him and Vasille was glaring at her for trying to create mayhem.

As the men joined them at the table, Coco excused herself stating that she needed to sleep and if they needed her just to call. She left the room dragging her feet heavily unable to shake the bad feeling inside her. If she didn't know better she would have thought it was because the girl was American but even Carlos and Quasi were strangers to her and it was their first time to deal with them, but they had been referred to Adhnan by someone special. She toppled into bed still dressed, her mind racing knowing she wouldn't get any sleep as long as her guts told her it wasn't safe, but finally after an hour of thinking and worrying she slipped into deep sleep.

A hand shaking the Arabic girl woke her up, the person standing beside her had kept their hand over her mouth asking her to be silent, shushing her. When she got her senses back and realized it was the American girl's she wrenched the hand away and attempted to yell so the American girl shushed her again.

"What is wrong with you?" asked Coco irritated.

"Get me out of here." Said the American girl her features rough.

Coco ignored her and fell back into bed, "Didn't Adhnan tell you that you can't leave?"

"He did, I just don't believe him" she answered.

"Go to sleep, if you want the sun to come up and find you alive."

"I am not threatened by them wolves!" Lorraine stated harshly.

"Then be threatened by me if I don't get my beauty sleep." And without another word Coco turned her back to the American lady and went to sleep, leaving Lorraine amazed on how anyone could turn their back like that and sleep soundly, with a stranger in the room and monsters outside it, *I guess you just get used to it, and I better start.* Lorraine then left the room like a spoiled child, stomping with her heels on the worn floor boards. Her audible racket woke Adhnan up and got him standing at his room door eyes half closed, his hair messy and his mood awful staring at her and asking "What the hell are you doing?"

"I can't sleep, you should be restless too." She said defensively, and again was bummed when he turned away and walked back to his mattress and fell in it.

Screaming out wouldn't have done her any good except get the wolves on her tail so she just walked back to her couch and hummed herself to sleep. Sleep that took its time to come, sleep that provoked salty tears she didn't bother to dry.

When morning came, Lorraine woke up and found no one as usual, so she sat there for a few minutes trying to accept the reality she was surrounded with but felt that she couldn't. She then got up and walked to the bathroom to splash some cold water on her face and over her hair trying to keep wits on her. She needed a plan and then a back up plan and then a ride to civilization. She stepped out of the room and out of the ruins they called home and into the blinding light of day. It's only when she smelled the oranges scent through the orchard that he wished she could reach up, grab one and quench her thirst with it. But she kept her eyes straight towards the gates and under the gaze of Adhnan and Quasi she walked out into the desert, and as she expected Adhnan followed her when she did not stop at the gates, asking her to come back.

She ignored him and kept walking and when she realized that he didn't follow her past that point, she smiled hoping that he had given up and he was letting her do what she wanted. But not long after she saw that she was wrong, he had revved up his engine and come after her. Stopping in front of her he took of his helmet and gave it to her and when she slowly took it he said, "I'll take you to civilization." As he turned away from her she saw the firm set of his jaw line and gulped but shook off the dreadful vibe she got, *she was finally going to see her brother.*

CHAPTER 8

When Lorraine glimpsed trees tops and houses over the horizon, she sighed inwardly relieved that this long hellish ride was over for many reasons. Not only was she going to run away like a jackal the minute he stops the engine, she was going to make sure she runs for her life like she had never done before. The only thing she didn't think about while making her plan was that the long ride would leave her legs numb and muscles cramped.

And the minute the bike glided to a stop inside the city, she unwrapped her arms of her driver's waist and started to jump of the seat finding her self unable to do it with grace and yelping as she found her muscles cramped just like after her first horse ride.

He just smiled at her when he saw her bending over resting on the bike before moving around the bike and taking her arm in his hand and pulling her gently along his side, she allowed herself to be lead along. She smiled meekly when he walked up to a cabin and unlocked the door, waiting for her to go in. She stepped inside expecting him to slam the door behind her and leave her but instead he gently pushed her further and closed the door behind him holding on to the key. The minute she glimpsed the bed she limped to it and sat down resting her legs for a minute before looking up to him and then cast her eyes down and asked,

"Why did you bring me here?"

"To rest, shower and get new clothes." He answered simply. She expected him to leave her but he stood there as if contemplating, then turned around and left the room. Seconds later he came back after a slight knock on the door.

"Is it necessary to lock you in?"

"Where are you going?" she asked her voice catching suddenly afraid that he will leave her.

"I will be around; there are clothes inside those chests. Take your time, can't promise you this luxury again soon." and before she could comment he added, "Don't waste time." and with that he was gone.

When he left she heard him lock the door and she gulped trying to remain calm, she hadn't had the time to tell him that she claustrophobic but even important she thought as she looked at herself, she was more terrified of germs. She jumped off the bed and started opening the chest for something that she could change into; picking a few pieces she threw them on the bed and walked to the bathroom slowly to check out its condition. She sighed in relief when she saw it was clean and even smiled when she saw flowers in vase on the window's small sill. She quickly opened the water and waited to feel the warm water rush through her fingers before taking her clothes off and jumping under it relieved to be able to get clean at last, somehow dying clean made her feel better about death and as the thought of dying crossed her mind her heart made a somersault in her chest and she broke into tears thinking of her brother.

Half an hour later she was lying face down on the bed in clean clothes and damp spirits; she had slid into light sleep and didn't realize that till she heard the key turn in the lock, she sat up slowly anticipating his entrance. She didn't dare smile when he walked in with a plastic bag; she gulped unable to decide whether that was something good in there.

Feeling slight pity for her, he handed her the bag without a word. He tried not to stare at her as she gobbled up her food her with her legs crossed as she sat on the bed, dressed in the black pants and shirt she had borrowed, and then drank the water he provided. It was amazing to him how she had trusted him; she didn't act suspicious of the food or of him and that relieved him somehow. He knew he didn't look scary like Quasi but he was capable of being just as aggressive. He sat on the floor by the door as she sat facing him finishing her meal, he had just decided to get up and sit on the opposite edge of the bed when she glared at him, he sighed and stood up again, "Do you want to sleep now?" he asked looking at his watch.

"I want to leave." was all she said.

"Do you have a place to go to?" he asked his eyes scanning her face.

"Yes, I can easily find one."

"That's not what I asked. This place is dangerous, you can get lost or shot. The probabilities of both are high."

"So if I stick with you I will stay alive?" she asked after a few seconds thought.

"Not saying that, just telling you it's not a good idea for me to leave you alone."

"You aren't responsible for me in any way." She answered with a smirk. "If I am going to get lost or shot with or without you then I'll save you the guilt."

"It's not about me." He said shaking his head not wanting her to misunderstand.

"Not the way you said it" she said "Anyways I think you are a thoughtful guy but that's not what I need right now, I need assurance and you are not giving me that so I will have to rely on myself, thank you very much."

"Where are you headed then?" he asked his eyes finally averted from her face.

"The same place you picked me up from." She simply answered.

Her answer aroused his curiosity, "What's there for you?"

Not giving him the answer he was looking for, she just said "That's the American embassy, isn't it? And as I am American they will be able to help me."

"Will you leave this country?" he asked without emotion.

"Yes, I don't feel safe plus I don't intend to get lost or get shot without reason, there are a lot of people here who use their weapons recklessly." she said pointing her accusation at him, but to him even if accusations flew he bothered only about the truth that he knew.

"Okay then, Good luck." He said as he walked to the door and opened it wide for her. She stepped back one step waiting for him, but the look in his eyes as he looked away from her to the outside made her move first.

She patted her hair once and walked out of the door, thanking God that she had comfortable shoes on for once, and said Goodbye.

He gave her a warm smile but didn't answer as she walked away and into the street under the heavy canopy ahead, she was a walking target and he knew he would be seeing her again dead or alive.

Adhnan then swung the door of the hut shut and walked to the bed, he shrugged of his coat and shoes and sprawled face down, the minute his face hit the pillow the scent of her body struck him making him turn the other side holding her breath. "Damn it Adhnan! This is the enemy you were talking to, get a grip." He let the air out of his lungs slowly and closed his yes thinking how hard it would be for him to have been the one to execute that beautiful woman, he knew Vasille would eat his head but he just couldn't kill her in cold blood. He smiled as images of her walking away crossed his mind, *now at least I don't have her around to distract me.* He rolled onto his right side and tried to sleep as he had a long day ahead back at the camp.

On her own again, Lorraine admitted to herself that she was a little bit terrified. She noticed people stare at her in her black clothes and red messy hair; she just hoped she would get to the Chad alive. She asked for directions and was given them with curious accusing stares. If she had any sense in her she would assume he was setting a trap for her but she would tell Chad every detail the minute she was by his side. She suddenly felt an awful pain in the pit of her stomach as the though of Chad being mad at her for what had happened, she would never mean to hurt him or put him through all that but it just happened but now she was safe and sound. She glimpsed the American flag on the top of a building from three blocks away, her eyes filled up with tears as she thought of her homeland. She dried them off and quickened her step towards the place she sought.

CHAPTER 9

Vasille nearly fell from his place atop the trees when he spotted the familiar figure of a red haired woman run gracefully through the yard. He cursed under his breath and put down his rifle which he was spying through wondering why Adhnan got himself involved with this woman, and when he looked back up to spy on her again she was gone. He knew there was no saving Adhnan from his conscious.

The young man climbed down and made his way hurriedly to the huts between the trees, where Adhnan promised him that he would take care of her, but obviously Vasille must have misunderstood. Steaming and more worried that he didn't defended him self against her and that Adhnan let her hurt him, even though that idea was so far fetched, he couldn't just rule it out and rushed to his comrade. The minute he spotted his friend's bike in the driveway he walked in not pausing to knock the door. He stormed in with his weapon up in front of him to see the man sprawled on the bed snoring, the impulsive man cursed under his breath and wished he could just shoot him. Truthfully, he was a bit relieved that Adhnan was okay but angry at how compromised they were at the moment.

Shaking the man to wake him up, Vasille called out his name and slammed his fist into the man's calf when he didn't budge. At that attack, Adhnan woke up yelping but ready to defend himself in case of another blow, but upon seeing Vasille he just dropped his body back down.

"What were you thinking man? How could you just let her go?"

"Why? What happened?" he asked his hand covering his eyes apparently trying to ignore his pain.

"I saw her run towards the American quarters."

39

"That's expected. She must have seen the American flag and knew it was the embassy."

Rubbing his eyes sleepily, he added "It's either that or she had been there before because she knows someone and is about to rat us out."

Sliding off the bed, Adhnan figured that he had better do something about the mess he created, and in fact he was frustrated at his own kindness. Now he didn't know whether to feel relieved that she was away from him or damn himself for jeopardizing them. He turned to face Vasille's angry stare and wondered how to tell him to leave the girl alone but before he could open his mouth a knock broke the silence.

Going to the door relieved for this interruption that could save his life from Vasille's murderous look, Adhnan opened it to see the very woman who was going to get him killed standing there. Vasille raised an eyebrow wondering whether it was luck or the Lord who was trying to save Adhnan's hide but he smiled at the prey that came to his door. He didn't move even though his fingers were itching to use his gun now held loose along his right side, it was only Adhnan who dared break the awkward silence, "What are you doing here?" his simple question was in more than one way accusing and comforting.

Gulping and giving a weak smile showing that she had no idea what she was doing, "I came to warn you. The military have located the house in the desert, I heard some guys talking so I thought I owed you a heads up for letting me go." her words only to her savior who was more pissed than thankful at that instant.

He pulled her in and closed the door before looking into her shocked face, "What did you tell them?"

"I didn't say anything, they did it by themselves if anything I came back to tell you that's what happened." she spun around to face Vasille's weapon, suddenly regretting that act knowing that she couldn't just walk out so she tried reasoning with them, "I was harmless when you let me go and I am harmless now, I didn't lead anyone to you and no one knows I am here. So I am going now."

But before she could step towards the door Vasille stepped towards her, she froze unsure whether to laugh or scream. She looked up at Adhnan for help but it seemed that he was unsure himself. She had already made enough stupid decisions for the day so she saw no harm in playing it safe this time.

"It's okay if you don't trust me." Lorraine said trying to be understanding but all she got from the man with the gun was a growl. "I had my chance for freedom and I came back so that should at least count for something."

She was being honest, she thought, because as she was entering the building to ask about Chad she heard two men talking about a solitary home in the desert with a ledge on one side and orange trees. She didn't need to think twice knowing that she might regret not letting Adhnan know that their location had been compromised, just for saving her hide. And now standing between those two men she wondered if she should have left things as they are.

She glanced at the door then at their incredulous faces and waited for the verdict, and before she could plead innocence again the weapon was down. In a matter of seconds Lorraine got dragged out and seated on the bike once more.

She tried to fight the urge to panic, but she knew it was futile to fight them. She contemplated jumping off the bike a couple of times but Adhnan's tense body only kept her in place. When they were out in the middle of the desert and above the noise of the engine he asked her, "Who is waiting for you in the embassy?"

Looking up at him, she only raised her eyebrows and refused to answer supporting his doubts. Both drowned in their dreary thoughts they got to the estate, where he found Quasi waiting for him with a package in hand. He went to the other room and opened it to find his fears confirmed.

Once he had cooled down, Adhnan sought out Coco because she usually had the latest information and updates on all unpleasant events. He found her in the kitchen mulling over a map and calculating things jotting down numbers in a small pencil. When he showed up in the doorway she gave him a look that didn't help release the knot in his stomach. He dragged himself to the chair opposite her and braced herself for what she was about to say. "Eman's men radioed. Their camp has been ambushed so they are on their way here."

He looked at her for a minute letting her words sink in. Emanuel Doma, his once brother-in-law was running a similar operation on a site not far from his hideout, secluded as well. "Did they have any visitors or did anything go down there that could have tipped the Americans off?"

"Not that I know of" was her answer. As she started to say something else the appearance of the American girl stopped her short, the stunned girl grabbed the pencil as she would a weapon and took one look at Adhnan and asked under her breath, "Why is she still here?"

Not in the mood for one of her fits he stood up and left the kitchen pulling Lorraine out with him, leaving an astounded look on both the girls' faces. He ran down stairs quickly not knowing where to go and what to do, but if he was to save everyone's hide he preferred to do it without worrying about whether the American girl will be stabbed by the Arab under his watch.

At the bottom of the stairs, he found Vasille waiting. His friend was standing with his back to the entrance, facing 15 men dismounting off their shining motorbikes, all new comers masked and armed.

One of the men in the rear stepped forward, he was bald and was dressed in gray denims with a long black coat. Unwrapping the scarf from his face to reveal a white handsome face and penetrating blue eyes, fringed with long lashes and a scar on his right eyebrow, he stomping in his leather boots and reached Adhnan in two steps taking him in a big hug. Adhnan kept one hand holding Lorraine's wrist and the other wrapped around the other man's body, "I am glad you are okay Eman, Coco just told me."

"You were out hunting I see" commented the handsome guy eying the American girl.

"No, it isn't like that" pulling the girl behind him away from the glaring eyes. "Let us go inside and talk. Vasille take care of the men, we might have a long day ahead."

Again inside the room, Adhnan let go of Lorraine's hand to have a private word with his friend. Vasille joined the conversation later and for the next hour they forgot all about her, as they discussed how the plans they had set to terrorize the Americans were turned against them. The thought of the possibility of a rat in their midst was out of the question but he knew there were glitches in their plan. It was too dangerous and wasn't practical to keep wrestling down American soldiers and staying low was time consuming. Eman and Adhnan were trying to come up with a solution or at a least a temporary delay to get the soldiers occupied for their own advantage. It was Vasille who was talking and explaining his point of view when the shrill scream had Adhnan out of his chair and out of the door, Eman just sat there stunned for a few seconds before he followed.

Furious that they were interrupted during their vital planning and with their lack of time and the massive responsibilities that were on his shoulder, Adhnan had had enough. All that of course was being topped with this beautiful innocent girl falling into his lap in the presence of a hellcat like Coco. He walked in to see Coco tormenting Lorraine, he reached for the Arabic woman who was holding a stick and beating the American girl with it, hauling her with one arm and pulling her away from the victim who had fallen down. He then bent down and aided the red head up and left the room with her. Adhnan helped her reach the couch she had occupied on her first day there.

He pushed away the hair covering her face and asked her if she was alright. His frantic eyes searched her face for scratches or cuts but found nothing, touching the blood stains on her face confused that their were no wounds behind them. She studied him as he searched her body for wound marks, her necks then her arms then his eyes rested on her hands. There were blood stains on her knuckles and under her nails, she raised her face slowly to look at him to see him glaring at her and without a word he stood up and walked quietly out of the room.

If there was such a thing as kicking one's self in the rear, this is exactly what he would have done. He had feared for the strange girl's life from Coco's brutality to be shocked that it was the American who had done all the damage. He went back to the room to find only the men standing at the window with their backs to him watching something below. Pushing his way through, he saw Vasille talking to coco with his hand on her arms pulling her back towards the house. Adhnan did not need to hear what she was saying to know that she was promising to kill her attacker, and like lightening he ran down to stop her. The marks on her face stopped him in his tracks. Horrified at Lorraine's acts and at his stupid emotions that had been steered the wrong way he moved forward slowly taking her arms by his hands and pulling her towards him "I am sorry Coco."

"Don't lie to me and don't feel sorry. I know you are not sorry, go back to that ...." covering her mouth with one hand he used his other to haul her over his shoulder in one swift move. When he got to the kitchen he put her limp body down on a chair, and turned his back to get the medical kit from the cabinet above the sink.

She cringed as she smelled the disinfectant and knew that the insult she suffered at this girl's hands was more painful than the stinging effect of the alcohol on her wounds. She turned towards Adhnan as he slowly soaked small pieces of cotton with the transparent liquid then gently starting dabbing at her wounds. She flinched and cursed under he breath as he cleaned the three obvious scars on her right cheek, and the small invisible one on her temple.

When he started to open the medicine lid she surprised him by laughing, "I am going to kill her, you know." And before he could react she was out of her seat heading upstairs, Adhnan usually had faster reflexes but her jump knocked the bottle out of his hands and he had tried to save the precious few milliliters left in it before pounding up the stairs where he found that American girl huddled on the window sill. And to avoid anymore cat fights he ordered Coco away and asked Lorraine to get down from the window threatening locking them up in a room till they learned to get along.

"You ought to lock her up in cage. She is damn wild." Lorraine said with a hiss still not moving.

"You are the one who ought to be locked up." hissed back the wounded girl "She was in the jeep radioing someone to come get her. After all you done for her she was giving you up."

"That isn't true!" came back Lorraine's sharp reply. "I would never jeopardize you."

Adhnan suddenly felt light headed and the room started to spin, he bent forward steadying himself with his hands resting on his knees unable to think, knowing well that they could be found by the radio signals, he was only able to imagine the whirring of helicopters above their ranch dropping soldiers. Straightening himself, he glared at the girls for a few seconds then turned and said, "We better leave. NOW!"

CHAPTER 10

Like a herd of gazelles preparing to flee from a pack of lions, the armed men prepared their shiny bikes and packed the food, clothes and ammunition that was stored in the ranch and headed out. Eman divided his men into two groups taking Quasi into his pack, leaving a few men with Adhnan to help him handle the two women, in spite of the presence of Carlos and Vasille.

Lorraine watched Eman driving through the orchard to where Adhnan was hauling boxes earlier, he motioned for the seven men he picked to follow him and soon the roar of the beastly motors was no more than a hum. Her stomach was in knots as she watched the rest of the men scurry around preparing themselves to leave. She watched Adhnan intently earlier as he and Eman discussed their situation, Vasille had glared at her baring his teeth like a wolf she had compared him to earlier. The angry man had been so pissed of with her that he had handcuffed her to the jeep's steering wheel. "Go on, call them in and we shall kill them one by one in front of your eyes." His fierce and vigorous tone made her shiver and tears arose in her eyes; blinking them away she started to say, "I didn't…" but couldn't finish it when a lump formed in her throat. Now staring at the metal restraints she wished she could scream loudly and bring in the wolves on them.

She wanted to know where they were going and what they were going to do, now that she hated herself for coming back to him and for trying to warn them. She should have let them die…all of them without exceptions. It was Coco and Eman that made Adhnan act different and cold, she bet anything that if she could get him on his own he would let her go. But it was hopeless with them standing around him, guarding him like he was the next Che. She lowered her head towards her knee trying to breathe sensing a panic attack coming on and that was the last thing she needed. After what seemed like an eternity in the scorching heat, Vasille came walking up to her, unshackled and pushed her in front of him towards the waiting bunch. Adhnan glared at him as he reached out for her steadying her, "Gently Vasille." He warned in a firm tone.

Then steadying her, he added "Coco and Carlos take the bikes and follow Eman, I will take the jeep, Vasille and I have something to attend to."

With a snarl the Arabic girl gave him the car keys and hopped onto her bike waiting for her followers to do the same, she silently prayed that the car would flip over and that only Adhnan would survive, she revved the engine twice before it came to life, leaving all who were behind to kiss the grit she splattered behind her. When the bikes have all vanished, Adhnan walked to the car were Vasille was to pat Vasille's back and squeezed his shoulder, "We have a long drive ahead. I need to be honest with you and you need to trust me." Vasille turned to look at his friend, "you can count on me."

Then without further delay Vasille guided the woman standing next to his friend to the rear of the jeep. As they both worked on replacing the removed top of the jeep Adhnan felt a sense of relief at having the courage to reveal the secret he discovered. When they were finished he threw the backpacks coco had prepared for them next to Lorrine, without giving her a glance. He jumped into his seat with one last look at the ranch house hoping that they wouldn't blast it once they found it empty. Suddenly, Adhnan remembered something they left inside that he needed to bring along with them, he made Vasille stop as he jumped and went to retrieve it. Lorraine's shoes and skirt were lying under the couch so he grabbed them, planning to throw them in the opposite direction of where they were headed. He and Vasille set off to throw the Americans of their fellow men's scent before heading back to the second camp.

Meanwhile Adhnan told Vasille the story of the girl sleeping in the back. He knew who she was and what she was doing here and was hoping she would come in handy. He explained to Vasille what an Ace card she was and that they had to take care of her, he confessed that he didn't predict how Coco would be jealous and hostile to the girl. Vasille was confused by his friend's explanation as he slowed down and stopped in the middle of the desert, Adhnan flung her things as far as he could and asked his friend to drive back. "We must catch up with them," Vasille sighed and shook his head as Adhnan glanced back at the girl nodding off in the back.

"You know you are gambling with her life." pointed out Vasille glancing at him interrupting his train of thoughts, "you knew I wouldn't like this and I wish you hadn't told me."

"So that you would think the things Coco is thinking?" asked Adhnan in disbelief.

"I trust you in this kind of thing but if Eman gets to know, he would have a rush playing with her life."

"Are you listening to yourself? It wouldn't make a difference to him, she is just an American to him. I love Eman and I trust him but he wouldn't understand that she is just bait. Not after what happened to Liberté." Vasille glanced at his friend uncomfortable at the mention of the dead girl's name and said, "How do you expect it to end?"

"With us winning and moving on from Panama." was all Adhnan said.

By the time they reached the city, hours later, Lorraine was up and drilling them with questions. She would answer them herself Adhnan thought, being the lawyer that she was, but the woman that she was wanted to piss him off. He was thankful to finally reach, the minute they parked among the bikes scattered haphazardly, he jumped out. He waited for the Texan girl to join him on solid ground, with his hands on her shoulder guiding her, he entered the first hut in front of him. Pushing her inside without looking at where she landed, then took a look inside the hut finding everything satisfactory he slammed the door shut locking her in. He needed a good night's sleep and locking her away was a good sleeping aid to him as any. Knowing she was safe and around was enough to knock him out for a few hours for sure, and with a hand gesture he signed to Vasille that he was going to get some rest.

CHAPTER 11

After a restless night, Adhnan walked out of his cabin just to run into his younger sister, the dark skinned girl with cropped dark hair and black dress smiled sweetly as she hugged her haggard brother. He held her tight for a few seconds before letting her go and keeping his arms around her he walked to the cabin they had formed into a mess hall. She placed herself across from him as he sat to eat his first proper meal since ages; he had taken to eating fruits and vegetables at the ranch to keep healthy and to stay light. She drilled him with questions about their future plans then moved to questions about the girl in the cabin, he didn't mind her curiosity because she reminded him of the reason he was fighting for a better country. By the time she mentioned the girl he had finished his meal and had been drinking his tea trying to clear his mind. He frowned at his sister and she mistook it for disapproval at the topic, but he had frowned because she brought the topic to the facade of his mind again and he started thinking about the American girl.

When Adhnan saw the concerned look on her face, he lightened his tight features and stood up and gestured for her to follow, on his way out he noticed Vasille sitting at one of the tables with Coco eying him without a smile. Adhnan ran a hand through his hair the way he did when he was unsettled and walked on ignoring Coco's glares. When they were out of the hall, Adhnan took his sister's hand in his own and walked to the foreign girl's cabin on the way telling his sister her story. And just like Vasille, she showed disapproval of what he had done.

Even though they were younger than him, their attitude towards the whole thing upset him. He knew that the whole idea of kidnapping the girl and using her as bait was wrong but not inhuman, for *all was fair in love and war.*

The minute they reached the cabin he took out the key he had strung around his neck the night before, and unlocked the door. Had she been any other hostage he wouldn't have been so guarded but he knew what she was able of, he asked his sister to stand away as the door swung open to the inside. Complete darkness and silence met him triggering his defenses, and just like he anticipated he put a foot inside and the strange girl swung something out of the dark at him. Alarmed he stepped back and as she charged forward, he quickly put his arms out to grab her flailing limbs making her yelp with pain. Shoving her inside with his body he landed her on the bed out of breath. The shocked girl in the doorway stood still; her hands on her heart trying to calm it, for unlike her brother she didn't anticipate the attack nor would she have been able to protect herself. The petite girl walked in slowly flicking the lights on to illuminate the scene, her brother was standing over the red head that was sprawled on the bed frowning and growling at him, with a bedside lamp in his hand, its beige shade torn and electric cord torn off.

Upon remembering his sister's presence, he asked her to go get some food for the American girl. When she was gone, he turned his attention to the American girl to see that she was trembling and he couldn't tell whether it was with rage or fear, but he knew she wasn't fit to talk to all the same. He kept his hold tight on the lamp, as he sat down beside her on the edge of the bed waiting for his sister to come. He glared at her for the sight his sister had to see, proving to him that this girl was going to ruin things and his plans weren't going to work. He wanted to explain to her what he was doing and why but he couldn't indulge his plans yet. Yet apart from his glare he didn't show her any sign of irritation, disappointment or anger. He wanted to threaten her but the determination in her eyes told him that she wasn't going to give in easy either and that made him smile in spite of his mood. Not the warm smile she had seen in their hideout but a smile that told her she wasn't going to make it alive and to that she frowned back digging her nails in the bed sheets under her. The unspoken cursing that was going on between them ended when the young girl knocked at the door. Adhnan walked to the door and swung the door open for her not taking his eyes of the hostile hostage.

"This is my sister," he said introducing the younger girl "Mera is most likely the only person you will talk to out here." he added, watching as the girl put the tray on the bed beside the American girl. He silently thanked God for Mera's common sense, for she did not place any utensils on the wooden tray except for a small plastic spoon. He smiled at the plastic plate and cup that held some hot tea for the girl, knowing that she couldn't hurt anybody with if she tried. He opened the door a little wider as Mera slipped out into the warm sun and he followed her for a minute asking her to go back and tell Vasille to get ready, they had to run an errand together. Looking to the inside of the cabin he found the girl standing at the window leaning her head on the warm pane, her food untouched.

He wanted to tell her to eat her food but didn't know what to say to the distressed girl, so he walked out locking her inside and leaning his back against the warm wooden door eyes closed. He wanted to capture the image of her face under his eyelids but instead found himself hostage to her beautiful green eyes and white cheeks. The poor man didn't need to look for a distraction for soon Vasille came stomping his way, accompanied by Eman. Adhnan gulped throwing the lamp towards his friend pretending to be clear headed as they discussed their next step in the plan.

CHAPTER 12

Lorraine had waited patiently for him to leave the room before starting to cry, she knew her attack would fail but she had to try. He hadn't hurt her when he held her arms and pushed her down on the bed, but the fact that he had anticipated her assault was shameful. She had never been aggressive in her life, but she had never been kidnapped before. Maybe trying to stay alive was a bigger task than she could handle, only she wasn't afraid of him and he wasn't the one she was defending her self from. The look in his eyes told her that his anger was a pretense and that he had to be this way around others to save her. She didn't know how she was certain; it was as crazy as trusting a timid wolf with your sheep but it was a wolf just the same.

She wanted to get to Chad somehow, she wanted to see him, wanted a chance to talk to him, she just needed him to know that she was well. Walking back to the bed she eyed the food hungrily and her mouth watered at the sight of the cooked chicken, unable to resist the smell she picked up the spoon and started eating knowing she needed to get some food into her system for the battle that was just starting. After she was done, she decided to waste time in the shower before going back to bed and conserve her energy. Her mind kept running the events of last few days in her head hoping to fall asleep. She didn't understand why it had to be her, why couldn't it be any other woman or any other man. *Did Adhnan already know about her identity and relation to her brother? Was that the reason he had chosen her? He kept asking her who was waiting for her, didn't he?* He probably didn't know a lot about her, but the most important thing is that he doesn't use her bait for Chad specifically. She got up and went to the door turning its knob, praying for a miracle, but the door was locked. She banged at it hoping for someone to open for her, seconds later she started kicking and yelling her anger turning into a tantrum, picking up a chair and hurling it at the door then at the window repetitively. Both objects of her assault didn't suffer a scratch then in one last attempt she hurled herself against the door before accepting how fruitless her actions were, she dragged herself back to the bed and sat with her head between her knees trying to regain composure. Minutes later she choked on her tears and slid down the bed curling up on the floor, tired and sad.

Meanwhile, Mera had been watching the poor sad girl from a slit in the cabin's wall. She hadn't meant to spy on the girl but she couldn't help but feel some sympathy towards the American hostage after hearing what her brother said. She didn't need to hear the screams that came with the actions to see the fear in the girl's soul. Mera wished that there was something she could do, because she had imagined herself in the girl's shoes when Adhnan had told her what he had done. She knew she couldn't open the door for the girl even if she had the key and she couldn't help but sympathize because this could have been her. The young Asian girl walked off when she heard her name being called, she figured Adhnan was back from where ever he was and she wanted to find out everything about his plans.

Reaching the mess hall, the Indian's young sister found him with Eman and Vasille arguing, she stopped in her tracks at the sight of the bald head she had avoided the many times he visited them, and the eyes she knew too well. She backed away knowing she couldn't open any subject in front of that rogue Adhnan called family. As she was turning away, she heard Adhnan calling for her again but she ignored him and walked past the cabins to the American girl's and sat by the door on the gravel knowing this was a good place to hide. But not before long the three men came walking towards her and knew there was no way she could escape them now. She smiled at her brother and Vasille ignoring the rude man with them, not saying no to the small hug her brother gave her as he reached her. He asked her to go to the mess hall and he would shortly follow her, sensing that he wanted to barge in on the helpless girl with his small army she whispered in his ear that he shouldn't go in now and not with them along. He gave her a questioning look but she assured him with hers and assured him that the girl in question was asleep. She squeezed his hand and pulled him away from the cabin and he followed to the amazement of the men who also followed him back laughing at how his sister could control him.

Mera thanked God that she had been able to convince Adhnan, although she knew that his friends would still be able to influence him and she needed to outsmart them. Not because she cared for the girl much but because she had felt bad for her and didn't want Eman to have his way with the hostage. In her eyes, that man was ruthless and had a lot of prejudice against Americans. The young girl tried to ignore his radiating hatred most of the time but there were times like this she couldn't help but shudder when he walked close by. As Adhnan headed to a table they sat for a meeting and since it was close to lunch time their comrades swarmed in interrupting the meeting, and it was adjourned.

Lunch was finished and the meeting recommenced after the meal over tea. Adhnan was pleased with what they have discovered; Panama City was having a party at city hall, oblivious of the dismay of the American's over the attack and the kidnapped girl. He hoped they would understand what they had been making people go through, and maybe just maybe, another unexpected attack on the Americans during the party would shake their soldiers and the traitor they want to place as ruler over Panama. The determined look in Adhnan's eyes encouraged Vasille who was shaken by the prospect of using a living girl as bait, but didn't show his fears and uncertainties. The only person who wasn't clued in and didn't need a reason to fight off the enemy was Eman, as he found joy in teasing Adhnan's sister, who was becoming more and more beautiful and more and more scared of him by the day. Adhnan and Vasille had their reasons for beating the Americans, but his reasons were bigger and deeper and his target wasn't just the fraction on Panamanian land but also America itself, and all the bully countries that wouldn't let the poor ones live peacefully.

As if sensing the hostile thoughts that were on his friend's mind, Adhnan removed his eyes from Eman's face and ended the meeting telling his fellowmen to prepare their weapons. He hoped that they wouldn't need to kill people more than the soldiers who intercepted them, they had made it clear no civilians were to die or get hurt, American or otherwise. With that he got a raised eyebrow from both Vasille and Mera and if he could see the angel on his right shoulder, he would have seen the same expression. He ignored them and tapped Eman's shoulder standing up and asked him to walk with him. Outside the two men discussed the attack and the way Eman wasn't paying him any attention got Adhnan angry.

"You know you can give us your input on this, after all you are going to be with us tomorrow and if you don't think the plan is a good sturdy one we can change it." Adhnan said trying not to sound cynical.

"You know that I don't like being played for a fool."

"Nobody does. Who is playing you?"

"You are, my brother." was Eman's simple answer.

Afraid to continue lying and unable to be completely honest, Adhnan smiled innocently and didn't answer. "You cannot possibly think that."

"I thought it only because you have done it to me, is there something you are hiding from me? Vasille knows it too because he cannot look me in the eye *brother.*"

Adhnan looked straight in his brother's eyes and grinned, "When you have a better plan of assault let me know."

As Adhnan walked away he knew that Eman wouldn't let it go, but he had to make tomorrow's ambush a success. He then changed his mind and turned back to amend the situation but Eman was already gone.

The Indian man had already explained to the men and women what they would do, he just needed to make sure they don't fail. As he walked to their "parking lot" where a dozen motorbikes were parked like a small dealer's shop he picked out Eman's dark blue BMW ride and started the engine heading towards the city.

Unable to foresee the reaction to his idea scared him, and as he ascended the steps at the city central police station, he prayed that the uniformed gentlemen inside would perceive things his way. Nodding to the guards standing outside he pushed open the door, and walked into the lobby that was more like an art gallery than the entrance to a secured police station. The only thing that General Noriega had done right in his presidency was allowing officials keep the right people in their right jobs. Every time he entered the building, Adhnan's breath was taken away over and over by the paintings. He would take a few minutes to stand in the middle of the foyer taking in the "horse paintings and orange orchards" illuminated by the light coming from the glass dome, and because the skies that day was clear and the glass was clean the paintings seemed to be coming to life bringing a smile to Adhnan's face softening his worried features. It was moments like this and talent like that which he wanted to protect, it was what restored his faith in his actions.

CHAPTER 13

"Adhnan welcome!" greeted the chief.

"Adunis, good to see you" Adhnan smiled shaking his handsome friend's hand. It was a pleasant coincidence for Adhnan that the Police Chief sitting across off of him had a name that started just like his own, and was also against the regime America had imposed on them and wanted change.

"How are you?" the Indian man asked smiling back.

"I am well, To what do we owe the pleasure of this visit?" he asked smiling back, "Have a seat please."

After both men had sat down, Adhnan gave the official the details of his plan. Adhnan, with Vasille and Eman came up with a trap that needed the cooperation of some influential men. The fiesta that was to take place would take place to spite the Americans, and bring the soldiers together like blind mice to a trap. What frustrated Adhnan most was that they weren't even on their land and they were not defending something that was theirs, they were just meddling in other people's business and property.

Adunis explained that the party would take place in the central hall and that Adhnan could place his men where the Americans could be trapped. Adhnan knew a lot of people would be volunteering to aid in the "fake" party, but he needed the cooperation of one girl. The police chief nodded as he listened to what Adhnan had cooked up with his men but he was a little bit unsure of how it will go down.

"I don't know Adhnan. I don't want to risk people's lives by using civilians as bait." said the policeman interrupting Adhnan.

"I have particular bait I want you to permit. She is an American girl I took hostage, her name is Lorraine Venus."

"Venus? Anyone related to Captain Chad Venus?" asked the Panamanian man shocked.

Adhnan nodded trying not to smile as he felt that his idea would certainly go through and he would get the permission he was after. He watched as the man sitting in front of him started wringing his hands and cracking his knuckles, "You are holding a very dangerous card and a very expensive one."

"I might never have played with a person's life before but I am an honest player and let's say I know when I am holding a losing hand but this is a winner, trust me."

"This isn't a one man's treasure we are after, you are taking about lives of a million people and a country's independence."

"I am not telling you that I am going to grant Panama instant independence, but I am definitely going to take the first step. Something has to be done and we must do something drastic. If not us then who, if not now then when?" his tone starting to get sharp.

"I can't allow this Adhnan, not officially."

"I need you to permit this; I don't want to do this without your support."

"I want to support you man, but this is serious. You have my support but it is not enough to allow you to do such a thing. My superiors won't be happy."

"You just permit it and it is going to go smoothly."

"I will let you know, is all can say."

"It is going to happen tomorrow, so I need the permission now."

"Come on, don't do this. Be patient, you will have other chances to ruin them but let us do it right."

"I see that I have done the right thing by telling you. Only regret is that I should have told you after it was done, to seek forgiveness and not permission. Now all I need is your blessings, good bye my friend and thank you."

Unable to argue, Adunis shook his friend's hand as he stood up to leave, holding Adhnan's hand in a firm grip he said, "If you are going to do this, I must take part but I beg you to rethink about it."

Adhnan gave him a half smile, and squeezed the chief's hand assuring him that if anything were to happen he would take blame.

As the Indian man left the building he took one more look at the paintings and rushed out to drive back to the camp before dark. After a quick drive to the market, Adhnan grabbed a few things the lady might need for the party tomorrow, after all she was going to be the center of attention in more ways than one. When he reached the camp, he jumped off his bike and ran into the mess hall seeking Vasille and Eman just to inform them that they might have to do this by themselves, without governmental support. After greeting the men in the hall, he looked around and saw no sign of his partners. Still with hot air in his balloon, Adhnan ran out searching for them but got distracted by a scream from the right side of the camp, without missing a single beat he held tightly to the bags in his hands he sprinted toward the direction of the screech. When he saw the American girl's cabin door wide open he dropped the baggage and sped towards it in panic. Inside the cabin there was no sign of the American girl, or anyone else. Adhnan paused for a second to catch his breath and figure out where the screams were coming from, when another came from behind the trees, he jolted and turned around focusing his attention and energy, rushed towards the sound.

A few meters away, he found the American girl tied to a tree with Eman towering over her holding a fist of her hair in his hand, his other hand tight around her jaw obviously hurting her. Adhnan rushed towards them in disbelief, to pull his friend of the foreign girl trying not to let his anger blind him. The girl glared at Adhnan as if it was his fault but he ignored her and pointed his accusing finger at his friend, "What is this you are doing?" not raising his voice at the bald guy took a lot of effort from the angry man.

"I can't believe you didn't tell me she is Venus' sister, I am going to kill her then gut him. Have you turned traitor when you saw her legs?"

"Emanuel! Shut up before you say something you are going to regret." warned Adhnan.

"The only person who is going to be regretful is you. You have signed her death certificate when you brought her into the plan. Vasille told me everything, or should I say I took it out of him. He isn't more honorable than you, he is probably with your sister, God knows where and God knows doing what."

"You better walk away." and with that he turned his attention to the girl and untied her and pulled her along with him, "This is the last thing I expected from you."

"Expect more my brother." threatened Eman, but Adhnan walked away ignoring him.

When he reached her cabin, he helped her to the bed and went back to get the bags he dropped outside, hovering over her he hated himself and guilt started eating at him again. She closed her eyes, her lashes wet with tears that she had just started shedding, holding her sides in pain. He thought that he had better get Mera to take care of her. Knowing that he shouldn't believe what Eman told him, he still needed to find Vasille. A sickening feeling rested in his stomach as he walked out and locked the door behind him with his key and suddenly wondered how the door had opened, seeing only slight scratch marks by the frame. He shuddered at the thought of being late and finding her dead, then he wouldn't know how to redeem himself in front of his Lord, he might be a kidnapper, a devious plotter, a swindler, a thief but he wasn't a murderer at all. Unlike Eman who wanted everything to be his way and no other way. This wasn't a game to Adhnan and he wasn't ready to compromise or forgive his friend for what he nearly did or what he said about his sister and Vasille.

Storming around the campus, Adhnan found them in the parking lot amongst the motorbikes, hurrying to his friend who was on a bike explaining the way to ride one to the young girl. The angry man grabbed his friend by the lapels and dragged him off the bike and punched him two times before hauling him up again and slamming him into the ground. Unable to regain his balance even once, Vasille didn't get the chance to defend himself or ask what was wrong. All out of breath Adhnan stopped and stood over his friend who was bleeding and lying motionless on the dirt. Mera, who was watching the one side fight, gaped at her brother in horror. He then raised his stare to her and beckoned her to get close, when she did the young girl put her hands on his arms trying to cool him down.

"So that you relieve your guilty conscious, you nearly had Elle killed." then turning to his sister, "Leave him here like a dog and go attend to Elle, I need her to look good for tomorrow's dance. I'm going to finish this with Eman."

"Don't please, Adhnan." She asked holding on to his hand. But he just pulled his hand away and walked away in strong strides his blood still boiling, his fists throbbing with pain and his knuckles grazed by his friend's face.

Eman wasn't actually hiding from his friend but he was in the last place he thought he would find him, in the driver's seat of the jeep parked in front of the mess hall, smoking a cigarette. When Adhnan reached the jeep, his target dismounted and stepped away from the vehicle his hands up smirking. Adhnan knew he couldn't fight with him in front of the other men, unlike Vasille, so he asked him politely to get back into the jeep and when Eman refused, Adhnan only had to show him his bloody grazed knuckles as a warning of what happened to his first victim to make Eman put his hands down and step into the car again. After they had driven for ten minutes, Adhnan stopped the car among some trees and got down asking Eman to follow.

"What are you making a big deal out of?" when he faced him on solid ground.

Adhnan didn't answer but kept glaring at him not knowing how to explain to him, without sounding bias.

"Adhnan,I have known you for a long time and I have never seen you so worked up over something, let alone a woman."

"It's not the woman." Adhnan answered slowly.

"I know that. Tell me something I don't know."

Eman's cool attitude was ticking Adhnan off and he didn't want to explain or give any excuses, he just wanted to punch his friend's light out. Advancing towards Eman, the enraged man swung at him but missed.

"Stop acting like a bull and listen to me. What is so special about her?"

"Even if she was nothing or no one, you shouldn't have hit her, this is what you don't understand" turning around for another attack.

"I knew you were hiding something but I didn't expect a woman to make you lie to me." Eman accused avoiding the blow.

"It's not about her, how many times do I have to tell you? She is important for our plans; she was supposed to be in the dance tomorrow. And now how do I make her look like she wasn't touched -just like I intended mind you- when you have maimed her today? How do you think her brother will act upon seeing her bruised?"

"And why didn't you share this last piece of information with me?"

Adhnan licked his lips and answered "Because of this! because you are rash and vindictive. If I had told you she is Venus' sister what would you have done? Slaughtered her like a sheep on the first day of Eid. It's not like I don't understand you, I just know what you think and how you deal with things. I needed to do this without your impulsiveness."

Eman interrupted him saying, "You forgot that I could have given you my insight on how stupid a step it was."

"Why? To add your vote to Vasille's and Mera's? no thank you."

"You don't think I want tomorrow's plan to work out? I wish we could blow them all up but you should have let me in I would have planned it better."

"Damn you Emanuel for thinking this is all about tomorrow. Adunis didn't even officially support it so we are doing it on our own and he said it doesn't have to be tomorrow. We could do this any other time I am sure, we can find other opportunities to get them but now and here you need to stop acting the way you do and especially towards the Venus girl."

"Admit it you are only feeling guilty because you kidnapped her and you planned this and if it had been my captive, and I was beating her up day and night you wouldn't have interfered and would have ignored the situation. So man up and admit it!"

Adhnan who was now resting his back against the car exhausted, closed his eyes, "It is true but you are not making this easy. I would trust a pack of wolves before I trust you with her life." Then Adhnan heard his friend laugh with gusto and stood up ready to attack again, but Eman put up his hands against the murderous look his friend gave him, "I am sorry for ruining your plans and am ready to amend in any way possible."

"Get yourself a tux; you are going as her date." And with that spiteful request he left the car and his comrade and walked back to the camp.

CHAPTER 14

Lorraine was awake when Adhnan entered the cabin to check on her, but she didn't turn around however she only assumed that it was him. She sensed Mera, who had been watching over her, get up in a hurry anxiously. Closing her eyes, she held back a sigh afraid that the foreigners might hear it through their low tone squabble. When she heard the door close she still didn't move because she could hear the faint breathing of someone, she let out her breath in slow movements, her chest barely moving, her exhaling just barely audible. The Texan girl squeezed her eyes tighter as she felt him move around the room and coming to stand at her side. He gently pulled the covers over her, unintentionally touching her cheek and to that the sleeping girl involuntarily cringed from his touch and he apologized. She heard him pull a chair and sit close by, not saying a word. With the even sound of their synced breathing she fell sleep and he followed in example a while later with a smile on his face.

When she woke up the sun was high in the sky and he was still in his chair, but he was holding a blueprint in one hand and a cup of coffee in the other frowning as he glared at the outline. Frustrated at having no privacy and no control over what these hooligans were doing to her and what they had planned for her, she huffed and puffed turning in the bed noisily. When he saw the way she acted seconds after waking up, he knew he had to smooth her mood up so that tonight would go well. He put the things in his hands on the small worn out chest of drawers and walked to offer her a cup. When she smelled the coffee, she sat up and accepted it without lifting her eyes or acknowledging his presence till she finished the drink with smile, and then just like she had suddenly noticed him in the room she said, "Must be a high price that I am going to pay for this."

Gazing at her beautiful smile shyly he said, "I told you, your fare and food are on me." Even though the truth was that they had stolen whole bags from some Americans some time ago just for laughs. He kept his lips sealed, and just took the cup from her and made a note of getting her a refill every time she got moody; he personally thought coffee was the best thing the creator had created, even compared to women. When he heard her move he turned to see her pull back the covers over her head and that made him yell, "No! woman, get up now!" but the girl didn't move.

He sprinted to the bed and snatched the covers away, then he grabbed her by the arm to sit up, but with that movement her deep green eyes met his dark ones and he suddenly felt weak and for a whole minute all the struck man could do was gaze into them as if they gave him a high. Scared by his silence the redhead didn't move and didn't even blink till he came out of his one minute trance, and when he did, he let go of her arm and asked her to get out of bed and change, as he pointed at the white stack of clothes that Mera had brought for her early morning. He took his map and left the room flustered as he locked the door behind him.

This time she didn't kick at it or bang, she knew it was closed for her protection form someone like that bald savage, she sighed and dragged herself to the bathroom and turned to gaze at her devilish state, with tears welling in her eyes she asked herself *What would Chad do ?*

After a quick shower and change of clothes she turned to the mirror to comb her neglected hair and braid it. She sat by herself thinking what she could do to make her imprisonment as painless and as short as it could be. She knew from what she heard from Chad about surviving in enemies' camps to be somewhat cooperative, except she never heard of a prison that let you shower daily and provided coffee. Ironically had she had met Adhnan anywhere else, his ethnic charm would have intrigued her for Lorraine knew what it was to be strikingly different.

She was lost in her thoughts, but snapped out when someone knocked at the door and the key turned in the lock. She smiled unable to keep a straight face as he came in, as if she were waiting for him to take her out to dinner.

Adhnan stood there stunned for the second time that afternoon in spite of himself, when he saw her sitting cross legged on the bed in the borrowed dress with her red hair braided over one shoulder, he got flustered again. All this was put aside when he saw her smile, her beautiful lips curving graciously lighting up her face. Looking away, Adhnan couldn't help but laugh at himself as his heart skipped a beat; clearing his throat he beckoned to her to follow him. And just like a kid promised a treat she jumped out of bed on her long slender legs bringing herself by his side instantly. Standing next to each other, the two strangers seemed to be of the same height, her gaze meeting his earnestly and all he could do was lose him self in her green gaze in spite of himself.

Thankfully Mera stepped in past her brother distracting him, bringing serious matters to his mind, and when he woke up from the enchantment he took Lorraine by the elbow and walked her out leaving the door wide open. They walked to the mess hall, but knowing that all eyes were on her; he took her to a far corner and sat her down asking for food to be served. She ate silently as he talked, listening to him as he told her what would happen today and once his mission was done she would be reunited with her brother.

She gave him a look that told him that she didn't believe him driving him to give her a smile; she would believe him eventually he thought, so he repeated the plan just to make sure she understood her role. All she had to do was be the bait and they would take care of the rest. He was just about finished with her when Eman came waltzing into the mess hall bored, but that mood quickly changed when he saw his most recent prey. Adhnan watched tensely as Eman proceeded towards them in the hall like a lion on the hunt, taking his time. It wasn't his advance that put Adhnan on edge; it was the smile on his friend's face that kept him alert. When she saw the way Adhnan's visage tensed, Lorraine didn't have to turn around to know it was Eman.

Watching Eman's reflection in Adhnan's eyes as he came close, made Lorraine grab her dish and utensils just in case she needed to defend herself this time also. When the bald guy reached their table he greeted Adhnan as if there was no grudge held, and slowly without any fuss Adhnan excused himself pulling Lorraine along leaving Eman standing there hurt.

Adhnan then escorted Lorraine to her room and locked the door when he left, worried about the events of the upcoming hours wondering how it would all fall into place. Walking around trying to clear his head unable to sit still or even drive around he finally came to the lot where all the bikes were parked, their shining bright skins had been dirtied for the night's mission reminding him of how everyone was in this and there were no runners. As he was looking around he took a cigar from his pocket and started to light it when his eyes fell on a bike that was still clean. He abandoned his cigarette letting it fall onto the dirt and started towards the mystery bike, his exploration was interrupted when he sensed someone prowling around, hand on his dagger Adhnan stopped moving waiting for the sly person to approach. To his surprise, none other than Eman walked up to him with a sinister smile on his face, "How are you my friend?"

Adhnan hesitated a second or two before answering, "what is it?"

Reaching out to his friend, he laid a hand on his shoulder, Eman said "I am well when I know you are still on our side."

Removing Eman's hand Adhnan said "Spit it out, Emanuel."

"The girl you have inside…tell me about her.

"Just an American girl bro who we are using as bait" Adhnan simply stated.

"Now…Now Adhnan, the least you can do is be honest with me" Eman answered chuckling.

"You already know who she is. What are you saying?" Adhnan asked.

"If she is indeed Venus' sister, you have done all of us a favor, and if you don't want her blood on your hands, you keep her way from Coco, for she is one vicious female."

Losing patience with that girl, and with Eman's insinuations, Adhnan said, "Your target is Noriega and we are using Chad Venus, and not his sister."

"I haven't forgotten, I just hope you remember that, and once we are done with Noriega I have a score to settle with Venus." He said giving Adhnan's cheek a light tap and walked away laughing.

Adhnan knew he had done wrong by kidnapping Lorraine but was certain that if Eman had gotten to her first he would have killed her. At least he wasn't responsible for her presence here in Panama, only for her presence in this camp and close to Eman. Running back to her room he decided to stay by her all times, and to him getting rid of General Noriega was all that mattered, despite of what Venus had done.

Time flew by quickly and night time finally came, Adhnan soon was standing in front of the hall with Lorraine, Vasille and Mera by his side, facing his team. Taking in a deep breath he sent two by two as a couple inside. Each couple was as prepared the way Vasille and Mera were, loose clothes for the men to hide the firearm and a flowered dress for the lady, where her weapon holster was attached to her thigh. The only men who wore shoulder holsters were Eman who had Coco on his arm and Adhnan who finally decided to stick to Lorraine for her safety. The three couples reached the entrance with the weight of the mission heavy on their shoulders, the responsibility of keeping their fellowmen safe a must, serving their country the goal.

CHAPTER 15

It wasn't the first time for Lorraine to go to a dance, but all the dances she went to were at huge houses, where girls like her flaunted their wardrobes and their smarter company. She looked around the hall, the modest interior and the plain walls only decorated by the colors and sparkle coming from the lit chandeliers. The floor was covered by thick red carpet and large flower vases at the corners with red roses inside. The vases in the hall were painted white and blue while the ones they saw in the lobby were painted gold and white with the same design and drawings and the same amount of crimson roses. The windows were draped with thick red curtains as were the chairs scattered in the waiting area, and she noticed that it was all antique furniture as per color and design.

As she twirled around the room in Adhnan's arms, after an hour of arguing that she couldn't dance, she sighed at the fight she obviously lost. She was impressed with the effort done to make this get-together look like a real party; they couldn't certainly think that this would pass over Chad's head. The soft music receded and a loud Spanish number started playing so Adhnan led her to the refreshment table at one end of the room, the farthest from the door. She stood there refusing his offer of a drink, her mask lifted off her face her arms crossed tightly across her chest. She shuddered as the image of Chad entering the room, and seeing him shot dead in front of her eyes as she stood there helpless. She couldn't believe that she would be bait and she would be the reason he would walk right into an obvious trap. Not all Adhnan's masked comrades were dancing and having a good time, some like Eman and Coco were eying her wickedly from the other end of the room while others just stood pretending to be shy people feeling out of place.

He tried to coax her into having a glass of juice to relieve her stress but still she wouldn't take it. So when he stood behind her and put his arms around her his chin resting on her neck his cheek barely touching hers, "Are you imagining us all vanishing here in front of you?" he asked huskily.

"This is the last place I imagine myself to be." She answered honestly

"Let's just hope your brother comes and this ends well."

"Please don't kill my brother." She requested in a hush tone.

"We are not after your brother to kill him."

"Maybe you aren't, but your bold friend threatened he would." And with that she turned around and placed her hands on his arms grabbing at them desperately, "promise me that you will help me and my brother get out safe. I will be indebted to you for the rest of my life."

"I would love to help you and believe you, but I know the minute your brother gives you a dagger you will stick it in my back." Placing one arm behind her back and the other hand lifting her chin, "but I promise you that your safety will be my priority." Holding her in his arms he swayed with her and she closed her eyes trying not to cry.

Adhnan felt her tremble and he pulled her closer burying his head in her soft neck smiling for a second before lifting his head and noticing Chad Venus enter the room. It could have been the way he stopped swaying or the way his body tensed that made her look up and turn around to see the familiar face of her brother.

He let her partially out of his grasp but he held on to her arm as she stepped towards her brother involuntarily. Chad Venus entered with a dozen men, the couples on the dance floor split and walked towards the walls acting as if they were scared civilians, knowing that the men who entered were not here to dance. The Americans had crashed the party pretending to maintain peace in crowded places, but to their disappointment this fiesta was slow and there were no out of order drinkers or problematic rascals. They scattered around the room but Chad who still hadn't noticed his sister stood by the door agitated, flicking a lighter on and off.

It was early evening when the Americans walked in, and what Adhnan, Lorraine and everyone else didn't see yet was that Chad was losing his mind over his sister's kidnapping. After a couple of clashes with Colonel Tanner, Chad was forbidden to talk about the search for her and so went out and about on his own whenever he could, contacting his comrades in different cities because he felt that they were putting her case on hold in fear of risking the presidency of General Noriega. He knew that he was to stay loyal to his country and career but his sister was his flesh and blood, and giving up on her search would be impossible. He was ready to give up anything in the world just to know that she was safe, and there was no doubt that he would confront Tanner again and again until he was sure there was no more hope or way that she was alive.

It wasn't till one of his prowling men noticed and recognized Lorraine that the moment of silence ended and all hell broke loose. Just as the American pulled out his weapon to point it at the man holding onto the redhead, Chad noticed and his eyes went from the pointed firearm to the target. He couldn't see the specified target as all the couples looked the same, till one man moved and his sister stood out form among the group.

Unable to control his rage, not even his disbelief could slow him down as he swung his rifle and aimed it at the end of the room calling out her name.

Lorraine who had instantly turned away and hid from her brother's view was too scared to be discovered. She didn't want to be the bait nor the cause for a fight, in spite of Adhnan's promises and his guarantees; she couldn't lure her brother into this trap. So Adhnan did the only thing he could he grabbed her to face him and with a straight face he took her arm and pulled her close, "I didn't expect you to chicken out." And before he could reach for his weapon he heard her name being called out.

Both turning around fast, they found a rifle pointed at them by none other than Chad. Lorraine's happiness that her brother had found her was quickly overthrown by her anger that his rifle was pointed at them so hastily. She tried to pull her self out of Adhnan's grip but he tightened his grip and pulled her by her hair to face her brother's aim. When Chad realized that he couldn't shoot at the man who was holding her, he put down his rifle and walked closer. The minute he took the first step, all bystanders who had been watching silently took out their weapons and aimed it at the Americans randomly. Eman, who was delighted at the success of the trap, walked up to the captain and degraded him off all weapons. The cold stare Chad gave the audience was an underestimation of his hatred, he didn't believe that he had gotten himself trapped like this and refused to accept the fact that the dirty rebellions had gotten to him through his sister, taking a glance over her side he saw that there was no weapon aimed at her head but only the kidnapper's arm around her waist. The relaxed stance of her frame was betrayed by the anxious look in her eyes, it made him turn his head away as he was asked to kneel and to place his hands behind his head. It was more of a humiliating stance than an execution position, for Eman wasn't going to shoot Chad like this; he had a more gruesome death arrangement prepared for the American.

For Lorraine the world had started spinning and she couldn't breathe, she didn't know what to do. All she could see was her brother dying in front of her eyes so she backed into Adhnan' embrace afraid of looking into his eyes and whispered, "You promised me remember?"

She didn't expect an answer but she knew that he had heard her when he gulped and cleared his throat and then with one move he pushed her forward and walked with her to the other side where Eman was holding her brother under the firearm still.

"Do we tie him up?" asked Eman.

"No need." Adhnan answered. As Chad's eyes met the kidnapper's through the colored mask he gritted his teeth. Then gesturing to Coco, he asked her to keep her weapon aimed at the girl while he stepped towards the captain and knelt to say that they want him to bring the

General down if he wanted to see his sister alive again. Eman knew that it was a good idea and knew that Chad was obviously concerned and ready to get his sister back. Ready to take serious action Adhnan motioned for the dancing couples to disarm all the American soldiers and asked Vasille to take them to the cellar down stairs. Adhnan had planned all the events and had only shared them with Vasille and Eman, Coco and the other fighters didn't know that those American soldiers were going to be taken down and locked in the wine cellar as Adhnan's army took over the hall. Chad was the only person to be released and would be given three days to convince his superiors to stop backing up General Noriega, and if he wanted to see his sister again, he should do a pretty good job of convincing.

Chad knew that not only his sister's life but the other ten men he led here were going to die, and he felt the importance of doing what these rebels wanted. When Vasille had returned after locking up the Americans, he was given the position of being Chad's point of contact. They wanted to bug Chad but Vasille assured them that they wouldn't need to worry, he wouldn't miss a thing. Chad stood up and looked over to where his sister was motionless standing and the lady still pointing her gun at the scared girl, as if feeling his eyes on her, Lorraine had lifted her face to show him the tear tracks on her face. On seeing her fear for him in her eyes, Chad smiled, in spite of himself and looked towards Eman and asked, "Can I just hug my sister?"

Eman snorted and waved with his gun to Chad to leave the building while he still could, as Vasille moved forward between Coco and Chad to lead him out, Chad moved aside trying to get to his sister Vasille used the butt of his rifle and gave Chad a blow in the belly and another on his head, and Adhnan who didn't see that coming was too late to spin her away, and could only watch her reach for her brother appalled.

"Leave now Venus, make this is as painless as you could for yourself and the others." And with that Vasille picked him up and shoved him through the lobby and pushed him out of the building and closed the door.

Unable to breathe for a minute, Chad fell to his knees and tried to calm his ringing head. Then the wounded captain staggered back to his office, Chad had to hide this incident from Tanner otherwise he would not even be able to save his men, without doing the impossible they asked for. Knowing there was no stopping Noriega now nor would he be able to save his men after the three day were over, Chad wanted to die of shame. He didn't understand how he was responsible for Noriega's presidency or Tanner's stubbornness. The only thing he was thankful for was his sister's safety and the fact that she was alive, despite the rags she was wearing and the tears that tainted her face, it was clear Lorraine could make it through the next few days.

CHAPTER 16

When Chad entered his office, his only ache was that in his head but when he saw who was waiting for him, his heart constricted in his chest. But other than the tears that threatened to well in his eyes, he tried to show the woman he loved that there was nothing wrong. Morena Tanner, didn't give him a chance to speak as she rushed into his arms crying. Holding her tight he tried to comfort her and asked her to stop crying because asking her what was wrong was only intensifying her sorrow and all she gave him for answer was more tears.

It was the first time that Morena came to visit him alone and so he assumed that there was a strong reason for disobeying her father, "Chad, you must save me please."

"What is sweetheart? You need to tell me." But all he got from her were more tears. "You need to calm down…shush…talk to me sweetheart."

"My father…wants me to marry General Noriega."

Had she taken a knife and ran it through his heart he wouldn't have felt it, but the words she said went right through his body multiplying his ache.

"That is not going to happen" he tightened his hold on her then pushed her away to look into her eyes, "That is not going to happen, do you hear me?"

"I can't live without you, what am I going to do?"

If Chad had any doubt about his career ending that day he was definite about it now. And if he could go back and live it again he wouldn't change a thing, for today he discovered that his sister was alive still and that the woman he loved wanted only him. His answer to her question was to pull her close and kiss her in attempt to stop her tears. "I want you to act like it is all right and that it is all okay, when the time comes I will come to you and take you."

"What are you going to do?"

"Leave it to me baby, I will do what it is needed, all you have to do is stall your father. You are mine, do you hear me?"

The scared girl nodded weakly as he dried her tears with his thumbs, "I love you Morena."

"I love you too." She answered and with that she said good bye and walked out leaving Chad a giant ball of anger. He could understand them rebels wanting to double cross him but for Tanner to take Morena from him that wasn't going to happen. He loved his profession, his sister and his Morena and the three of them were slipping out of his hands, if he couldn't save the first he had to try and save the rest.

Pacing around his office, Chad wanted to disappear just like the rest of his team so no questions would be asked, if his team was missed they would be thought dead but if he was to roam around without them, doubts would be raised. So taking some maps and things he figured he would need, and replacing his stolen guns with others in their holsters, he left the office. Looking around for the last time he took a deep breath and walked out slamming the door loudly.

Throwing his backpack he had filled into a jeep he was about to steal, the angered Captain drove away from the safe world he knew, heading to the only place that would welcome him in this God forsaken country now. At the park projects deep in the desert, the weather was colder and images of finding snakes everywhere made Chad's skin crawl as he dismounted form the jeep. Before he could grab his stuff, the familiar face of his friend Johnny came out of the window of the small caravan smiling and eager.

"Chado, man you are here!" Johnny called from the window to his friend and slammed the window quickly before jumping out to greet him. The fit jock jumped down the steps in his khakis' and green shirt, his green eyes wide with excitement at this guest who hadn't come in a long time. The deserter smiled at the warm greeting from the friend he missed, the friend who had been transferred to the projects after pranking his seniors and embarrassing them. *More of a punishment for me,* thought Chad, *as his friend Johnny showed no regrets.*

Shaking his comrade's hand, Chad felt at ease at seeing Johnny again and when they went inside Chad dropped his bag and walked directly to the cabinet, where they hid the liquor. Pouring some for himself not including his friend, he downed a drink after another as he built the courage to tell his friend what he had done. Watching him, Johnny crossed his arms over his chest and waited for his friend to look his way anxious at what he was about to hear. He was used to Chad dropping over every once in a while but wasn't used to seeing him be the first to drink as drinking was Johnny's thing. When Chad had put down his glass he turned to his friend smiling, "Don't worry buddy, I wont finish it now because we are going to have a long night ahead."

"What is it Chad?" he asked moving forward to take the bottle from his buddy and put it aside.

"I have not drunk enough to confess my stupid mistake or to reveal my dim witted plan."

As curious as Johnny was, he was more concerned now but decided to let his friend be, "Come on, let me show you around man, they did a lot of new stuff around here."

The project was all about adding life to Sarigua, and making it bigger and broader. Johnny was like a Texas Ranger on Panama's soil, but without his fellow Texans and with time he got used to it. After hours of walking around the desert land aided by a flashlights and the full moon, Chad saw that it still needed a lot of work, hectares of sand that could get you lost easily if you didn't know your way around.

"You know I have done more stupid things than you ever will." Said Johnny uncomfortable with his fiend's silence, when they settled around the camp fire they made. As they sat preparing their simple dinner, the two friends drank coffee silently.

All that he got from Chad was a smile, still unable to confess to his friend, wanting to stand up and fix all that went wrong straight away but just like how he didn't know how it all went wrong, he didn't know how to make it right.

"Even you wouldn't do what I had done." He said whirling the remains of his drink in the tin cup held in his large hands.

"Let me be the judge of that buddy, I want us to get this over so we can start having fun."

"Even if I tell you, it won't get fixed tonight." He sighed eying the bright moon wishing he was on it.

"Is it your girlfriend?"

Chad snorted but didn't say a word, trying his friend's patience knowing that the earlier he shared his shameful secret the better it was for him and the faster Johnny would get over his shock and they would start making a plan.

"No way!!" was the host's first reaction when Chad had finished his story. "Jeez Chad, you sure surpassed me this time dude." Wanting to laugh but the graveness of the situation made him swallow it. "Let me get this straight, so you lose your sister, and when you find her you lose your team and if you don't get things done the way those rebels want, you will lose them and your woman?"

Chad knew there was no point in nodding, he only frowned because the way he put it wasn't kind. Not that Chad needed someone to soften the blow or make it look peachy for him, it was going to be black as night and even crimson as blood that he was going to be responsible for, if any was shed.

"You are not going to sit up all night to make a stupid plan are you?" asked his host.

"What do you mean?

"There is nothing to think about, its either you raid their lair and get your sister out. Or you raid Noriega's home and kill him or threaten him."

Taking two cigars out of his breast pocket, giving one to his friend and then lighting his on the bonfire careful not to hurt himself, "either way I'm going to need Tanner or am I going to be screwed."

Johnny sprawled back on the dusty ground, his cigar unlit in his mouth contemplating, gazing at the clear sky above him where the stars were shinning and twinkling. He sighed thinking that it was a shame that on a night like this there was so much to worry about, poor Lorraine God knew how she was doing.

Lorraine's brother however, closed his eyes trying to digest what he had seen in the afternoon, for it felt like a lie. His sister couldn't be dressed so neatly and be so clean and yet be captive. He had seen the way that man had his arms around her waist and the way she stood in his embrace. He couldn't understand why she had to come to Panama, his anger returned as he thought that none of this would have happened if she hadn't come, he wouldn't have disobeyed Tanner, and he wouldn't have lost his team. Knowing that even without her incident he was going to lose Morena, at least for that he would simply kill Noriega. For killing or hurting the colonel would be his loss, and Morena would never marry the murderer of her father, but by God it was impossible to swallow the reality pill!

He was considering the raid on the rebels part but wasn't sure what he would gain. And he didn't know if Lorraine would still be in their lair or the jungle, it just didn't make any sense. He stared into the fire listening to its sound as he sat there surrounded by the cool night air, its rhythm interrupted by his comrade's snoring. He envied the sleepers that night for their peace of mind; he thought it would take him long before he could have forty winks again but as soon as he had placed his head on the ground he started snoring himself.

CHAPTER 17

The Texan girl, who was on the other side of town, had no difficulty sleeping after she had cried all her tears. It was bad enough that she was not released herself but rather she had ten new inmates now, and if it would have solved anything she would have killed herself and ended the hostage situation that had her brother distressed. It was as if she had shattered her brother's world in all meaning of the word, Chad couldn't do anything to Noriega unless it was illegal and it was impossible without his team. *Maybe not very impossible if he were to go on a suicide mission,* it was a sad and frustrating thought, and just like the movies, she was ready to do anything even go back in time to fix this.

Unlike her brother, the disturbed girl didn't sleep soundly; she kept having nightmares all night and was turning left and right unable to sleep well. And when Adhnan came to check on her he found her asleep on the floor of her room curled up onto herself. Even though the floor was wooden he was afraid that she would get sick so he got down on his knees to pick her up. She merely stirred in his arms as he placed her between her sheets, her hair brushing against his arms causing him to hold his breath. Covering her rapidly, Adhnan sneaked quietly out of the room and closed the door behind him before letting out the breath he was holding.

He knew something drastic was going to happen because of the event that they had prepared the night before but he also expected the Americans to have a counter attack. Now winning was complicated for either party, as it all was in the American captain's hands. He had faith in the man, looking at it from Venus' point of view, having your sister and your men' fate counting on you, it was enough to break any man but Chad Venus wasn't any man of that Adhnan was sure.

Leaving behind the object of his affliction Adhnan stepped away from the door and headed to the mess hall. He knew that if he talked with Vasille and Mera or Coco; one was bound to knock some sense into him. He knew they had to see this through to the end, Eman's way or any other way didn't matter, Noriega had to leave.

Lorraine had to leave too, was they all told him as he sat with them for breakfast the next morning. He imagined losing her smile that tugged at his heart, he would never give her up he feared unless he was heavily sedated or tied when doing that. He enjoyed protecting her and the way she glared back at him when he glared, the young man wished that they had met under different circumstances. He knew that it was all in his head for she surely wouldn't even give him a second look had they crossed path any other where.

Finishing of his coffee, he excused himself and walked out of the mess hall even more confused than when he walked in, it wasn't time to let his heart race and skip heartbeats and yearn. It was a shady state of affairs and in this race against time it was either him or her brother. He was ready to give her up once was Panama was free but if he could keep both, he would, *provided that it was mutual.* He was under the assumption that it was only his head till he saw it in her eyes, the minute he knocked and entered the room she jumped out of bed and ran to him eager for news. When he shook his head and told her nothing had happened yet, her eyes filled with tears and she rushed to the bathroom slamming the door behind her. He wanted to go in and comfort her knowing it was still early for any updates but it would have been useless, she had a lot to lose. He waited patiently at the door like he knew he would have to wait a lot from now, accepting that silently if not painfully.

When she came out he was gone but the door was left wide open, she walked to her bed and lay down looking at the world outside, she contemplated leaving and walking away, but how far would she reach before reality caught up with her and brought her back. She was lost in her thoughts when he came back with food, he wasn't sure she would eat but he figured the look of some toast and the smell of coffee would bring her back to life. Hungry, she ate but without interest, and what got to him as he sat watching her is how the glow around her had started to fade ever since she had come and how if she stayed under these circumstances the twinkle in her eyes would diminish too, and she would no more be Lorraine and what would be left of her is an empty shell.

He didn't know what to say and didn't know what to do, he had to wait like everybody else to see what Venus would come up with. Like a falling domino the step that American would take would either send them downhill or towards freedom and not necessarily side to side. Before he could make a move Vasille appeared at the door and told him that Eman had come into the mess hall asking for him. He nodded and got up without a glance at the woman who was bound to break his heart and test his loyalty.

Somehow the brilliant idea and sophisticated plan he had formulated was turning to be a fail on his part and just like a wild flower, it would entrap and kill him. Where he went wrong Adhnan didn't know, he had seen people being kidnapped before and ransoms and conditions asked, with things going well for the kidnappers finally. And that was the thing that terrified him, he was no kidnapper and nothing could pardon his doings, *who was he to kidnap and scare an innocent girl? To use her as bait, to terrify her, or to threaten her brother's life and to have Eman belittle hers?*

There was no use sharing any of this with Eman because the French man had every intent to ruin their lives, to him those Americans are as good as dead, and it tore at Adhnan's heart. He didn't know what had attached him to Lorraine other than the fact that he felt responsible for her. It was a heavy burden and it was unbearable, and got worse as he walked into the hall and saw Eman carving at the wooden table with his blade. Biting his lips, and aiming to keep a straight face he greeted his friend and sat across of him ready for a private fight between his head and his heart.

As Adhnan figured, Eman had a plan and had come to explain it, not long after Adhnan was sitting explaining it to Vasille and Coco, finding him self faulting every step and every detail. Coco stayed behind when Vasille left to check on the American soldiers, watching as Adhnan was torturing the cup he had been drinking coffee out of, she moved to sit by his side and took his hands in hers. He gave her a skeptic look when she smiled at him, but when he saw the look in her eyes he rested his head on her shoulders. "This isn't time to let your heart wonder for she isn't your type my dear."

"Isn't that what you said about Liberté?" he asked whispering the dead woman's name.

Expecting that question, Coco's smile broke into a laugh that brought tears to her eyes. "Liberté was a different story, I had my reasons to say that."

Finding it easier to talk with his head down and eyes closed, he answered "Liberté was my everything, and nothing will change that. Eman knew I loved his sister and her death was inevitable but I know he will never forgive me. Stop trying to win my heart Coco." Sitting up to look into her eyes, "You might have to start thinking about where you are going once we are done here." He said taking his hands out of hers and bending down to kiss her forehead then walking away tears forming in his eyes over the memory of his wife.

He left the mess hall with no intention of going to Lorraine's room, but found his legs leading him there. When he realized his route he stopped, and turned round, then turned towards her room again. He told himself that coco was just being ridiculous and he was feeling nothing but sympathy for Lorraine Venus. That effort was gone with the wind when Mera came walking up to him from the car yard.

"Brother, how are you?" She said as she reached him, and put her hand on his shoulder.

"I am alright. Where have you been?" he said pulling her close.

"Went to scout the embassy with Vasille, but then he said he wanted to go scout further and look for the captain while it is light, so I came back" She said all innocently, raising his eyebrow at the thought of her being with his friend alone but didn't say anything to her, he must have not gotten to Vasille the first time.

"What are you doing?" the young girl asked when she saw him walking with her aimlessly.

"Going to see Liberté" he said in a matter of fact tone that made her stop in her tracks.

"What?" she asked shocked.

"What?" was his response when he realized what he had said.

When his sister gave him that I-am-worried- about-you-look, he shook his head and said, "Not you too", leaving her and walking away into the trees ignoring her calls.

CHAPTER 18

Sprawled on the hood of his Jeep, Adhnan closed his eyes and tried to shut everything out. but the harder he closed his eyes, the clearer the silhouette of a tall woman became. Reaching out for her and pulling her close, he rested his head on her body and surrendered to her warmth. The woman smiled, placing her hand on his head and playing with his hair, she rocked him gently, humming a lullaby in his ear. Holding back his tears, the young man fought his sadness as he asked her why she left him all alone. The time he spent with her was short, but he believed he could do anything and be anyone in that short while. All he wanted was to have her in his arms again, to hold her and love her, to have her children and love them, raise them to be Lord fearing and strong men, serving their creator before their country.

He had so many dreams and so many plans growing up but when he met her she became his dream and her future his objective. Liberté, the light skinned tall girl with high cheekbones and long hair was the object of his affection for the while he knew her in, although his young age and hot blood had always driven him to be restless urging him to keep living for his family. He never even considered marriage for at that time he assumed it would drive him away from his sisters, until he had met her and changed his mind. Had it been love or infatuation or just respect for her, he would never know, all he knew was he couldn't approach her without her brother's permission, and putting a dozen obstacles in front of himself, he decided that she was no good for him and he was no good for any woman. He knew that all they would want was to settle down and have normal lives while his conscious would never let him. And just as if to spite him, fate had made her different from every other female on this planet, that he couldn't but ultimately find his other half in her, leading him to ask for her hand from her brother Emanuel, so she would eventually be his. Trying to suppress all good memories was impossible because she appeared in each and every one of them, and he wanted her image to stay in his mind in spite of his aching heart. Love was a small word for such a great girl; he often believed that she was exchanged with an angel at birth... a*n Angel that heaven took back.*

He didn't know how long he was out but when he opened his eyes, he opened them to an angel's face. He closed his eyes again effortlessly and let his dreams devour him again, but instead of brown eyes and a dark hair, he saw a green eyed gaze and crimson tresses. A frown creased his tanned forehead as he tried to recollect his wife's face and the more it alluded him the more scared he got. A cold touch on his warm face made him open his eyes abruptly, his eyes wide with apprehension to see him staring into the American's girl face. He gazed back at her trying to recollect who she was and what she was doing, and when it registered in his mind his muscles relaxed, and before she could see his bewilderment he sat up and turned away composing himself.

Minutes later he turned around to speak to her but was stunned to find himself alone. He jumped off the hood of the car and walked around it, listening for her steps walking away but heard nothing. Bending forward and leaning his weight onto the vehicle, Adhnan took a few deep breaths confused and afraid that he was going crazy over a woman again. Getting down on his knees he waited for his dizziness to go away, telling himself that he couldn't allow himself to become weak, not now, not over this woman in particular.

Standing up and running his hand through his hair while walking around trying to get himself together, the young man figured he had to self preserve before he self combusted. He didn't know why he had become so weak after promising himself to never forget how the last time he let a person matter to him, that person died and he had lost half his soul. But he was a believer, and he understood human nature and the Lord's ways, and if it had to happen with Lorraine Venus he prayed to the Lord it wouldn't end with either of them dying. Trying to get his act together he walked back towards the huts straightening his hair, once Lorraine's huts came into view, he strutted towards it and knocked on the door, before barging in.

Letting the door swing open expecting to see the red head there, the Indian man was disappointed to see the room empty. Just then a loud laugh rang in the air, recognizing it the startled man moved towards the trees led by his sister's laugh. Adhnan couldn't help but smile even though he had warned her a million times not to laugh so damn loud. His smile grew wider when he saw Lorraine with his sister Mera on the dirt their heads together like school girls discussing something, but when they saw him they looked up innocently he couldn't help but be curious.

"What are you doing out here?" he asked them in a light tone.

"I thought it would be best if she had some fresh air" spoke his sister adding an apology, quickly standing up and offering her hand to the nervous American girl.

Adhnan only nodded, asking them to be careful then he walked away his smile glued to his face in spite of him. He wanted to kick himself for acting like a love struck teen, but he knew he enjoyed the feeling too much to stop himself.

On his way to the hall, he ran into Vasille and they walked towards it to let Eman hear what Vasille had come back with, he had gone and spied on the Americans to find out that they were searching for Venus who had abandoned ship. He heard that they found him gone without a sign, him and his team, and were presumed deserters. They were sitting and discussing his whereabouts when Mera came running into the hall, calling for her brother, and when she spotted him she grabbed his arm pulling him up saying that the American girl ran away.

After understanding that Coco came around and scared the American girl, Adhnan swore under his breath and let go of Mera's hand and towards the trees he flew. He was not only worried about her, he was also worried about who she could bump into and that made him angrier at Coco. He reached to where he had left them and advised Mera where to search though he knew he would find her first in the most obvious place. Running towards the American colony through the trees looking right and left, he hoped to the Lord that he would reach her first. Not catching a glimpse of her all on the trail he figured that he had lost her and she was already safe in there. Leaning against the nearest tree his heart fell thinking that she had already walked out of his life, watching and waiting for a sign of her, clinging to some ray of hope but to no avail. In a way he was relieved that she was gone but on the other hand he was devastated that he didn't even say good bye.

CHAPTER 19

He wanted to go back to the hideout to get some work done only he knew he would not do a single thing, instead all he would be occupied with was her well being. *That stupid girl,* he thought, *no she wasn't stupid,* he corrected himself, because he knew she bound to run for her life at any given chance. It was his fault to start with and it was a mistake that had to be corrected, and it would have ended well if she didn't come back the way she did the first time. Shuffling back towards camp, he tried come up with many scenarios to tell his sister that she was gone and it was all good, but he kept looking back hoping she'd be at his heels.

As he had expected, coco, Vasille and the others were in the mess hall waiting for his wrath, but were dismayed to see him walk in with a sad face. She was a hostage and he was the rebel, she had to go and she was gone they understood that because it was logic. Only he wasn't listening to that logic as his heart was going crazy with worry over her. He walked out after a few words towards his room and shut the door throwing himself onto his bed, feeling horribly weak and sick.

He had hostages to think about, his comrades, Chad Venus and that coward Noriega. Closing his eyes for a few minutes helped calm his blood flow away from his throbbing heart and calmed his senses. The Indian man knew himself, he well knew his mind and knew that when he was disturbed by something, he had to resolve it. He knew that he was wrong and would probably disrupt their mission but he was responsible for that woman, he knew he was a point in his life where he had to let her go because she didn't belong among them. But in case she needed his help again he wouldn't hesitate a single second, he reassured himself.

The young man feeling restless, left his quarters and weaved his way through the foliage surrounding the camp. He pulled at the leaves that touched his fingertips as he edged his way through finding himself close to the waterfall, the spot he hated the most on all earth, that is why the minute he started hearing the sound of the water as it broke on the rocks below he froze in fear. It scared him to remember how the fall from the waterfall itself didn't kill but the vicious rocks down there where what broke any falling object in two. His knees got weak at the memory that he had to rest against the nearest tree trunk. He leaned against it, lifting his hurting knee on a bare root that was poking out of the ground, using it as a stool.

He rested his head, closing his eyes cursing himself for even coming to this place and before he could set his mind to go, his foot was kicked off making him yelp in pain as his eyes flew open.

"Dhat tere ki.." he said under his breath as he saw the American girl standing in front of him.

"Did you just curse at me?" asked Lorraine, out of curiosity rather than anger.

Adhnan sighed and said, "it is not like that." He stared at her unable to tell whether the pain he felt was from his throbbing knee or aching heart. He decided that he was hallucinating again until she spoke. "Why did you come back?" he asked, upset with her rather than curious.

"I never left." she answered simply.

"How did you know about this place?" he asked calmly.

"I didn't." The American girl lied through her teeth.

And as if unable to suppress it, the memory of the tragedy that happened one night at this spot, came rushing back to him. Lorraine watched the Indian man's features change and as if she could see the incidents unfolding herself in his eyes, a sense of fear gripped at her heart at the incidents that Mera had narrated to her.

"Adhnan, Run!" Liberté, his wife and comrade yelled running in front of the young man between the trees panicking, as Adhnan tried to stay at her heels. Rains of bullets flew above them and from the side as they ran fled from the Americans. It was dark and cold and all he had to lead him was the sound of her breath as she dashed ahead of him. His tense muscles kept pushing forward even when a bullet pierced through the back of his leg just above the knee. Tears fell down his face as the pain clawed at him but refusing to let Liberté know, and refusing to let her get hurt because of him he kept up with her till they reached the edge of the forest where they found an animal's hideout hidden by a tree's roots. The couple crawled in not caring whether there were dangerous animals waiting for them inside, and once there the wounded man stayed down out of breath and gripping his wound biting the inside of his cheek. His comrade was on the look out oblivious of his state until she smelled blood. Turning to see him sweating and bleeding, Liberté felt her spirit weaken and her courage beginning to fade. She knew that she had to throw the Americans of their scent if she was to save her man's life, so she approached Adhnan and held him close as he slipped into unconscious. She didn't want to say goodbye, but she didn't know whether they were going to meet again so with her throat burning and her eyes blurring she slowly took of his jacket and head band before laying him on the dirty ground.

"You believe in the afterlife, don't you boy?" she said, "Whether there or here let us meet again."

The tall girl crept out of the hole, putting on her husband's jacket and started running in the opposite direction hoping that the enemy would never find her man. Hours later Adhnan who was saved by Vasille, was looking down from the top of the waterfall at the body of his wife that had been shattered on the rocks below. He sorrowfully gripped his leg as he wished that it was his limbs that had been broken and not her fragile, beautiful body. He had walked away that day bleeding and defeated knowing he could never claim her body as he hoped that her soul was some where near him, protecting him as he vowed revenge for her.

"Come. I'll take you back." the wounded man said as he limped reaching for her hand.

"I have no where else to go." she said pulling her hand away. "Chad had left his post, apparently he could not find support for such a ridiculous mission."

"He will get it done, don't worry. I am counting on him." then as if expecting her to follow he limped away miserably.

The American girl followed silently as they weaved their way towards the huts, eager for this chapter of her life to end. But it would be so regretful if it ended and her fate with this man was cut, she didn't know why the more time she spent around him and the more she saw him she liked him more and approved of him.

"Do you believe in the afterlife?" he suddenly asked not looking back.

"Yes, somewhat." she answered, suddenly remembering why Lorraine stopped in her tracks in disbelief. She had totally forgotten about her daughter in the last few days, appalled by the change she had gone through in the past few days or ever since she had met those people, the Texan woman flopped to her knees weak and in pain.

Looking back Adhnan saw the woman on the ground shocked and unable to move, he knelt down beside her shaking her panicking, afraid that she had been bitten by a snake or something. When she looked up at him and apologized, he calmed down and lifted her up. Staggering beside him, he asked "Did I ask something wrong?"

"No." she stammered, wiping her tears, "I just remembered something. Something that I shouldn't have forgotten. I don't know if I believe in the after life, I just hope that there is another chance where I can redeem myself and pay for my sins."

"I don't know what you have done," the young man said, "but I believe that we are punished according to our intentions. Go back to that and judge yourself."

She could tell that these people were of a different belief as she had observed their lifestyle for a while now, and she could tell they were different as they prayed all through out the day and didn't drink alcohol. If she were to tell him that she had a daughter out of wedlock he would probably feed her to the wolves.

"There is someone that needs to be punished." she said "it is he, who is making life unbearable for my family. He has occupied our home and life, and has killed mercilessly. That is why I need to get back with Chad and save my family." she stared into Adhnan's eyes asking him to let them go.

The young man knew there was more to her story that she wasn't telling and maybe because she was afraid of being judged.

"I will come and dethrone him, once I dethrone this guy."

"I just need Chad to return well otherwise our whole household is doomed."

He wanted to comfort her but he knew that in this world, nothing was guaranteed and no life was without loss.

"Do you think I want you or Chad, or his team to be harmed?" he asked in disbelief, "the people you see here in the camp and our other comrades are also family. I lost my wife here in this jungle and my sisters are in this with me. Do you think it is okay for us to die if it wasn't an important issue? I only got involved because of my wife, but once she left it was up to me to get her dream moving forward. After her death I promised myself that I would never let another get hurt again, so we will all get this done with and go home." he said trying to assure her.

Assured, and believing him even when her mind told her it was a lie, she nodded and walked with him towards the camp.

As he was walking her back, his mind and heart were too occupied to sense the danger enclosing from afar.

CHAPTER 20

When Adhnan stepped into the mess hall, after dropping Lorraine at her hut, he was taken back by the tension in the air. The mood wasn't good and it showed in the way an argument was heating up between Eman and another comrade.

"What is going on?" asked Adhnan banging on a nearby table.

"It is about time you showed up brother," started the comrade, "I have found traces of intruders close to the camp but Eman brother wont let us move out."

He then walked over to place something in Adhnan's hand and looking at it Adhnan felt restless, "these are American cigarette stubs, I found them in two locations around camp. I know the chances are low that we have been exposed but the possibility is there."

"Let's clear out." was all Adhnan ordered.

Minutes later in spite of Eman's fits and insisting that there would be no need, the whole camp was packing up. Adhnan understood Eman, and knew it was hard to move to another camp that was already filled with their comrades but staying here with a risk he couldn't take since they were nearly at the goal.

"Adhnan," Eman stopped his friend by grabbing him by the arm as he was leaving, "we have ten extra people to take with us." referring to the American hostages, "we wont be able to move them with us."

"We will have to manage man, it's a risk we will take. We will leave in groups",He said walking away.

Adhnan walked out as Eman kicked a chair cursing Adhnan's stubbornness, when he walked out he saw that everybody was standing in the open space looking in one direction, when he turned his head he saw Lorraine standing at Vasille's gunpoint her arms up.

"Vasille man, what are you doing?"

"She came back! again! Who gets to be free three times and comes back?"

Adhnan frustrated walked to his friend and lowered his gun, "I brought her back. Let's move now and fight it out later." then turned to everybody else, "Go! Go! Go!"

The crowd dispersed but not before he got a few odd looks and head shakes from his peers, but Adhnan didn't care because all he had to do is remember his intentions and matters at hand.

As people started packing their weapons and food, as well as their mere belongings Vasille started splitting people into groups and into different camps. He did his part in preparing for evacuation with different thoughts messing with his mind, not knowing whether to stay with Eman or leave with Adhnan.

Adhnan let his angry friend cool before going back to the mess hall to try and reason with him, "you can stay here with some boys and hold the fort, we will move the Americans since Venus knows where they are."

Eman who didn't like to yield to anybody knew that the Indian man was right, so accepted but after drying Adhnan's throat. Adhnan didn't like to fight with his boys but when it came to his responsibilities and people's lives he never stepped down even if he ended up with a swollen face.

In a matter of hours, the camp was almost empty, and dust had settled in the wake of leaving vehicles. Vasille, Adhnan and a few men were left behind to tie loose ends at this camp before leaving it in Eman's care. Eman was hung on this camp specifically because it was closes to civilization where he got his cigars, and Adhnan had no intention of disrupting his friend's inner peace and he himself wished that they didn't have to dismantle their team but it was an emergency.

Adhnan cleared the air between Lorraine and Vasille, and headed to his hut for a short rest.

What was supposed to be a short nap, didn't last 20 minutes as he jolted up when he heard gunshots. When he opened the door to see what was going on, Lorraine flew inside banging the door shut and shoving him to the floor in the same instant.

"Its' a raid!" she exclaimed her eyes wide with fear.

Coming to his senses and up on his feet, Adhnan grabbed two guns and night vision goggles he had under his bed and handed her a pair. The Texan woman's hands shook as she accepted it, "I have never shot a person before."

"It's not the first thing you have not done before." he said putting on his goggles and prompting her to do the same. "save yourself first then worry about others, do you understand?" he said calmly as though he was explaining something simple.

Then opening the door slightly, he tried to locate the enemy by their rifles by their laser beams crouching down and crawling out of the hut hoping that the few bullets in his gun would be enough against their weapons.

CHAPTER 21

Lorraine was crouched in the mess shall when the shoot out was going on, and when it was over Adhnan found her gripping to her gun for dear life. He helped her up and walked her out to see that everybody was safe, messed up and sweating but safe. The huts however were damaged beyond hope.

Hearing the gunshots from inside was harder than being outside and watching how the fight went because with every gunshot and wounded man's cry she prayed that it wasn't Adhnan who was hit. When they were gathering the bodies that had scattered around, a sound of a jeep approaching got them on edge again, they hid themselves in the mess hall awaiting the intruder as silently a possible.

When the arrivals saw the bodies, their footsteps hurried to look for any survivors, "Adhnan! Brother where are you?" was the first sign to bring relief.

"Marroma!" Adhnan exclaimed and jumped from behind the counter without being careful. "What brought you here?" She hurried to her brother and hugged him with one arm, the other pulling her rifle back, "When you sent me your people, I felt that something had to be going on,. So I came to check. Are you all alright?"

"Yes," he said as he scanned the faces of his comrades who had come out of hiding, their injuries minor and their smiles broad welcoming the help that came to them.

Realizing that there was no need to hold this fort anymore, Eman joined the survivors and rescue team to continue his fight from a different base, hanging on to the only precious item he owned, his cigar case.

Lorraine stared intently at Adhnan's other sister, who was tall and beautiful. She had large eyes like her brother and their color of hair matched, her slender fingers brushed her brother's hair to remove things that had gotten stuck to it, arousing a feeling of jealousy in Lorraine that the Texan woman refused to acknowledge. As she moved her eyes away they landed on Vasille who's face had gone pale, "Hey, Vasille" she called out to him then moved over and slapped him across the face causing him to sit up straight and place a hand on his face yelping. It was then that she saw that his pain came from his arm that was bleeding so Eman applied first aid then asked him not to move it till they reached camp.

Vasille was the happiest with the way things turned out because there his sister awaited with her team, he grinned as she scolded him and treated his wounds with the least bit of sensitivity. When she was done they gathered around the leaders to plan the next move and catch on the latest on the American's agenda.

This camp, Lorraine noticed had more women and young men than Adhnan's. It seemed more like a refugee camp and Marroma a benefactor rather than a leader. Lorraine uncomfortable with the stares directed towards her, kept her eyes on Adhnan afraid of being abandoned now that he had more things to do.

The American girl got distracted by a meal brought to her by Marroma, who looked after her like she was a child, asking her questions while she ate. Lorraine could tell that her hostess was younger than her but she still kept her manners and showed respect to the woman who saved them. When she looked up Adhnan was nowhere to be found. She tried not to panic as she scanned the area with her eyes, she excused herself and got up slowly edging through the field towards the vehicles, upon hearing the sound of an engine her heart lurched in her chest. Lorraine sprung forward in time to see Adhnan and Vasille driving away from the camp.

"Adhnan!" she approached him yelling out his name.

"What? What happened?" he asked halting in alarm.

"Where are you going?" she asked nervous.

"I left some things back in the camp, I am going with Vasille to retrieve them."

"Take me with you." she said grabbing his arm.

"I am not ditching you. Stay with Marroma and I'll be back in a few." he said trying to keep her calm.

"I will go with you." she said showing him that she still got her gun and that she'd help him.

Uncomfortable with her nagging, and unhappy that he let Vasille wait, he closed his eyes eventually surrendering to her. As they headed out he tried not to get mad at her understanding that she didn't want to be away from him, but taking her was dangerous not to mention distracting.

It was a long way back but the path was clear and incident free. Half way they dismounted and preferred to complete on foot as the enemy was probably on the look for suspicious vehicles. Adhnan kept looking back to see if she was right behind him as she made no sound when she moved, just like a mouse he thought smiling to himself.

When they got to the camp that was no merely remnants of their good times, the Indian man went into his hut to retrieve his belongings. Vasille was outside watching for intruders while Adhnan was fishing through the mess that had taken over his room.

"I will go check for left over weapons, stay alert." Vasille ordered Lorraine, as he walked towards the mess hall.

Lorraine wasn't planning to go anywhere until she heard a familiar voice, her heart fluttered at the thought of seeing her brother, the Texan girl entered the hut to tell Adhnan two words before she left quickly, "I heard Chad's voice, I am going to see him."

Before he could stop her, the excited girl ran out calling for her brother. Knowing what dangerous thing it was considering that the voice she heard might not be her brother, Adhnan rushed after her calling out her name. Vasille came rushing out to see them go into the jungle not comprehending the situation, but feeling that he needed to follow.

Lorraine couldn't get very far before gunshots started flying at her and her savior, She stopped in her tracks when she realized that her brother could have joined a new team who didn't know how she looked like. It was too late for her to turn around and hide because the bullets that missed her had embedded into Adhnan's body. One had gone through his shoulder and the other was deflected by the satchel that he carried to slightly scratch his side giving him a flesh wound.

Both victims struggled for breath as they ran for cover in the vast jungle, Lorraine tried to pull him up and stay by his side every time he faltered, then when he fell to his knees she knelt in front of him to encourage him to get up. She knew that he must be hurting and frantic for her, she had to hide her fear and show him that she was alright. She pulled off the bandanna that she pulled back her hair with and used to push against his wound. He yelped but didn't get a chance to relax his head against her shoulder for soon the gunshots started again, he started to get up and pulled her with him and started running again, blood oozing from between his fingers but he ignored it. They had gotten a good distance away, so when Adhnan couldn't go any further because of his wounds and hurting leg, she helped him down in a well hid corner. He smiled as he wiped her tears with his thumb, but no matter how he tried to straighten his features, his face was too pale in her opinion. She was trembling in front of him, but holding herself pretty well.

"Why did we stop here?" he asked weakly.

"You shouldn't move anymore. You are losing blood."

"Staying here wont save my life." he said, "if anything it might make me lose you we have to keep moving."

"I will go look for Vasille. Hold on." she said pressing her bandanna into his wound making him cry in pain.

He placed his hand over her hand, "Don't go." and as if suddenly realizing the gravity of the situation her lower lip quivered and she started crying uncontrollably.

"I wont die. Stop crying." he asked her earnestly his pride hurting him more than his wounds, as he felt himself experiencing a deja vu. It made his head spin but he managed to say, "Vasille will bring help to us. Stay here."

The Texan woman sat there watching the Indian young man breathing with difficulty, sprawled against the tree hiding them from the world. She hated herself for tugging along in spite of his refusal. Also for running to find Chad even though thinking about it now, there was no guarantee that it was him. She would never forgiver herself if something were to happen to Adhnan she thought, for knowing how things turned out with his wife and how that woman ended up dead, it was all because Adhnan was someone who was able to sacrifice himself and compromise his safety.

Lost in her thought, she didn't see Adhnan close his eyes and start to fall asleep.

"Adhnan! Don't sleep." she pleaded turning his head towards her, "Adhnan stay with me please."

Opening his eyes slightly, he smiled and said "Liberté is calling me. I can't be late."

"Don't forgive me. I have done a terrible thing towards you. I shouldn't have come back." Lorraine said quietly while crying.

The weak man raised his hand and pulled her hand away, "Take the bag I am carrying, it contains your stuff. The stuff you lost on your first day here."

The distraught woman didn't understand what he was talking about, all she wanted to do was slap him to wake him up, but having him talk to her was enough for now so she kept provoking him to interact with her. Lorraine asked him to pray for their safety. Letting go of her arm and removing the hand that pressed against his wound, he lifted his hands slightly and started mumbling things she couldn't understand. When she saw his features relax and his lips stop moving, she put her hand on the bandanna and pressed a little, waking him up.

When she saw him get his senses back, she asked "Can you get up? Lean on me."

"Go. Leave." he replied.

"What?" she whispered in disbelief.

"If Vasille finds out that this was your fault he will not let it pass. I will hold on till he shows up. I promise. But I can't promise to protect you from him when he finds out."

"If I believed in another life where you and I would meet again, then I would have left you in heartbeat. But if I leave now I don't know how and when we will meet again."

"I am being punished for wanting to run away with you" he said suddenly losing his senses again.

Saddened by the way this strong man was going to slip from her Hands, she pulled him by the lapels and yelled "Don't forgive me, do you hear? If you don't forgive me then you wont forget me, make sure you look for me at least to get your revenge."

"Adhnan!" Vasille's voice broke her rant, as he got close to see them in their hideout, and the young man had never been more happy to see the red head.

"Vasille! Oh thank the lord, quickly come," she called out to him to help his friend.

"It is not so bad, it is going to be alright." said the comrade knowing that his friend was suffering because of his bad memories more than his wounds. "I will carry him on my back, you lead the way."

Freeing his friend from the satchel he carried then turning around to pull Adhnan over his back, Vasille hoped that the American woman would be able to steer them away from trouble.

Steering through the empty fields scared Lorraine because of the responsibility she carried on her shoulders. Things went smooth for a while until it started getting noisy, Lorraine stopped and pointed for Vasille to go down a muddy path.

"What about you?" he asked, concerned that Adhnan might blame him if he wakes up to find her not there.

"Some body has to be the distraction," she said going the other way.

"Adhnan will kill you if he finds out, come back" the anxious man hissed.

"Don't let him go to Liberté" with that Lorraine was gone.

Even though he knew she was gone, Vasille still yelled, "You better come back!"

Vasille fought the urge to run after her, he held himself back and left to save his friend. *She will come back, she always did* he thought to himself pretending not to be worried, not knowing at the time that it would be the last he would see her. He stood there waiting for her to come back from the jaws of death...

***

"Yup, that was the last time I saw you." Said Vasille with regret. "if I had known I would have persuaded you to stay."

"Why would you?" she answered ridding him of all guilt, "it turned out for the best, they were Chad's people, so technically I was finally where I needed to be, and you got to where you needed to be."

"Adhnan made quite a fuss and he waited for you until the day Noriega was sent packing, thanks to your brother of course. After that was over he dusted himself off and left Panama. He went back to France where he had first met Liberté and sent her away properly. I never thought he would let go off her memory but he even took off his wedding ring and moved on."

"If you saw him now, you would never believe that he was the same person. He went back to the academic world and is responsible for changing a lot of lives." added Marroma.

Before they knew the voice from the speakers ahead called the passengers traveling to Dubai to approach the gates, so with a heavy heart Lorraine said her goodbyes, and exchanged phone numbers with Marroma promising to stay in touch.

She watched with dismay as her friends walked away, and when their backs were no longer visible, the Texan woman picked her bag and walked away from the spot that she had occupied with them. As she was walking her attention elsewhere, she tripped on a bag's handle pulling the piece of luggage from under its owner feet.

"Dhat tere ki.." the person muttered in a low voice.

"Did you just swear at me? How rude!" she asked as he stood up and walked towards her.

"Didn't I tell you that it wasn't a curse?" Lorraine stared at the Indian man who was everything his sister said he was; clean, refined and smart looking that the Texan woman could only be dumbfounded.

"What is the meaning of this? Why are you here?" she asked still surprised, still unable to fathom how handsome and smart he had become.

"I promised to dethrone your tyrant, didn't I?" said Adhnan with confidence.

"It is already over, and we are at peace with the past and present."

"I have made peace with my past as well, I have forgiven myself."

"Have you forgiven me?" she asked sorry for the way she jeopardized his life.

"I forgive but I don't forget." he answered with a wink.

"That's a relief, isn't it?" she put in.

Then putting out his hand, he said, "I say since we are here let's run away together...though the last time you ran away from home it ended badly."

"Not really it didn't. But hey, fare and food are on you, okay?" she agreed putting her hand in his and laughed at her own joke, while he stared into her beautiful eyes helplessly and nodded.

Printed in the United States
By Bookmasters